THE GIRL WITH THE DEAD RAT

AANCHAL K GUPTA

INDIA • SINGAPORE • MALAYSIA

ISBN 979-8-88783-589-1

To my mother and father,

For always believing in me

I love you

(Aalok, my brother, I love you too but wait for the next one)

CONTENTS

ACKNOWLEDGMENTS

When I woke up on the morning of 11th August 2021, I had no idea I would start writing a novel that evening.

But thanks to some incredible people, I am extending my story to the world.

Firstly, I would thank my father, Mr Deepak Kumar, who believed in my passion. He researched publishing houses alongside me and guided me throughout my writing journey.

My love for the English language would be incomplete without Miss Surabhi Deherkar, my English teacher, who introduced me to the magic of literature.

Notion Press and its dedicated team provided the best services. My anxiety raced up high when I started looking for publishing services. But their team cleared all my imploring questions.

I am infinitely grateful to all my friends, who read through my initial drafts and propelled me forward.

I extend a warm embrace to my family for keeping up with my late-night writing sessions.

My brother, Aalok, would always have to sleep with the lights on.

Lastly, I would like to thank my kind readers, for picking up this book that has my words etched through its veins. I am grateful to you for giving me a chance to enter your synapses.

Thank you so much, this means the world to me.

I-11TH JULY 2021

Rainwater gushes around the window pane while Jannat silently stares at the thundering sky.

She wanted an island vacation, but who knew she would almost die having one?

"I found some fruits," Shaina cheers from the musty floor.

Finally, some nourishment for them.

Jannat looks around at the tear-stained faces, all waiting for help to arrive. Would they ever get out of this place? She wonders.

She wishes she had never done this.

II-2020

Green Lawn Central School

Mrs Sharma is heading towards her Chemistry lecture. The students greet her with their singsong tune.

"Good-Morning-ma'am!" they screech.

Although the kids have grown up, certain habits they haven't left. She silently stares at the class through her rimmed spectacles. A wave of fear rushes through the children.

"Children, today, a new promising student has joined us. Meet Jannat."

A seventeen-year-old nervous girl steps in the doorway. She is wearing the Green Lawn Central uniform, a crisply ironed shirt with a blue blazer and trousers as the sun shines on her innocent but stern face. Mrs Sharma welcomes her with a motherly nod.

"Good Morning. I am Jannat Resoulda. I am enthralled to meet you all. I like reading books, listening to music and swimming. I hope we all learn great things together."

A gentle swoosh of murmur sweeps through the classroom. Mrs Sharma registers one of her death stares as the children go quiet.

(If looks could kill!)

Jannat takes a seat beside Shaina, the class topper. Shaina straightens her glasses and gives Jannat a weak smile.

Jannat whispers, “Don’t worry, I will not take your top position away!”

Shaina coughs and manages to stare in shock at her new partner. How did she know her so well?

Mrs Sharma starts teaching Electro-chemistry Time passes as Jannat thinks of the real reason, she joined this school. She looks around and wonders how long before it happens.

III-2020

Same day- Green Lawn Dining Hall

Shaina purposefully marches towards a bustling lunch table.

"Oh! Look who decided to visit us," Ahmed sneers from the crowd.

"Guys, the new girl, Jannat, is weird," Shaina blurts.

"Shaina don't worry. She likes One direction too. She is safe," Roshini says with her palm facing forward.

"Are you people psychics? Is there a Professor Trelawney workshop that I missed?" Shaina chirps.

"No, we are Gen Z. We have Instagram. That's how we know vas hapennin. Look, she is from Punjab, quite an ordinary girl," Asha fills her in.

Shaina stares at the smiling faces and vivid memories in her hand. She loses balance as someone nudges her from behind. She gasps and turns to find out it is the very person she dreaded.

"Wow, ok, is that the new Harry Styles song video because I am feeling golden tonight," Jannat jumps in with her food tray.

"Hi, Jannat.Nice to meet you. I swear I wasn't stalking you," Asha buzzes, retrieving her phone from Shaina's grasp.

"It is ok. I swear I wouldn't have wasted a second to stalk a public account like that," Jannat snickers.

"Are we just going to keep making Mr Zuckerberg richer or eat something too?" Ahmed protests using his cutlery as a weapon.

"Oh! Look who came in with the low-key Nerdy joke. Also, that knife makes you look like Ravana," Shaina snarks while helping herself with a gulab jamun.

Ahmed grunts with his face full of food.

They eat in silence for a while. Shaina constantly keeps scrutinising Jannat and accidentally stabs a samosa. Her eyes study each subtle move made by Jannat. All those Sherlock Holmes novels she had read were finally paying off. Jannat offers her innocent smile to the predictable opponent. Ahmed is deep down in his meal when Roshini interrupts the tranquillity.

"Hey Jannat, when did you move here?"

"It's just me here. Family is back in Punjab."

"Oh! So you will join us in the hostel," Asha exclaims while clapping her hands with playful mischief.

"Umm...Yes!" Jannat says after swallowing some paratha.

"Well, there are some rules. No sleeping before ten and pillow fights every Saturday. Be careful, as the pillows have a very less thread count," Roshini adds with a cheery yet diplomatic smile.

"I have already paid fines for five bru-tah-lee destroyed pillows," Asha says with her eyes so vast that her pupils visibly contract.

"She means brutally," Ahmed jumps in, trying to save their first impression.

"That's how Principal Mehta likes to describe them," Asha revolts back, justifying herself.

"Woah! I know, whose team to be on, then," Jannat giggles.

IV-11TH JULY 2021

"Help arrives soon, Miss Jannat," a cold voice answers from the old clanky device.

"But Sir, we are almost starving here," Jannat pleads.

"You know the policies, don't make me repeat the conditions. Everyone has been through this," the man replies.

"And died, at the end. So, easy for you to write things and make people follow them."

"Stay within your limits, Miss Jannat, or else!"

"What can you do, Sir? Kill me! I am already dying. It already kills me to see these poor faces suffer every day. It Kills me to keep lying to them. All my life, I have been lying. No more; this is enough now."

"You know the terms your father had laid. I think you love him enough to follow them. Goodbye, Miss Jannat.

V-2020

The girls' dormitory

Jannat settles on her suitcase, wondering how to manoeuvre the overflowing beast. Roshini assists her with the luggage.

"Aaaah! Why does this suitcase get constipation every time?" Jannat scowls.

"Hey, look, we have a hiking trip next week!" Asha exclaims, holding a pamphlet.

"Yayy!" Roshini lifts her hands to cheer. The suitcase explodes while Jannat gets projected above.

There is a loud thud on the floor, with Jannat landing safely like a squirrel, proceeding to pose like the Black widow as she amplifies her stance.

"How did you do that?" a curious Shaina asks, enunciating her head movements with each syllable.

Jannat looks around while thinking about how to answer that. Lost for the right words, she says, "Some self-defence training and active reflexes, there you go!"

In a desperate attempt to divert the attention, Jannat smiles in relief and says, "Why don't you guys tell me about yourself while I unpack?"

"I am Asha Shinde. I love photography, memes and hedonistic people. My parents work for the charity that runs the school. It gives me access to some confidential information," She says while doing the air quotes.

Roshini excitedly jumps, uttering, "Oh yeah! Asha always has the best gossip material! Well, I love reading just like you. I also enjoy nature, writing and cooking. Well, not so much cooking, but eating for sure."

"Sounds cool. Could always love some foodie company," Jannat snickers while placing a photo frame beside her lamp.

"Darjeeling has some of the best momos. Some warm thukpa on a winter day. Oh boy! That's the best," Roshini chimes.

"Shaina, your turn," Jannat says while adjusting her planner.

Shaina shifts in her seat and clears her throat. "I like painting and studying, as you may know. Food has never been my forte. I like roaming the streets and getting along with the buzz and chaos."

Jannat nods while Roshini keeps wondering about those momos she had last week. Asha is swatting a fly from her face when Shaina interrupts.

"Who are the people in that frame?" Shaina mutters.

"This is my family. My mother is a software engineer. My younger sister, my father, the bravest human I know," Jannat adds a weak smile while trying to stop the pool of tears from descending her cheeks.

"Hey! I thought you were the bold bee ready to get the nectar," Asha adds, giving Jannat a gentle pat.

"How many other Instagram bio's, do you know by heart?" Jannat smiles with her wiping her twinkly eyes.

"We need to give Jannat a good tour of the city," Roshini comforts the newcomer once out of her momo fantasy.

Later that night, Jannat shuffled into her bed. She is dreaming of the unfortunate night that changed her life.

The cold voice fills her brain.

She gets up, panting with fear Beside her, the girls are fast asleep. Even the restless Asha seems to be snoring softly. She thinks of how long before these soft snores and peaceful minds disappear.

VI-TEN YEARS EARLIER

"Aarav, I want you to come back. We have no resources to keep funding you," mutters the cold voice.

"Sir, we have all their access codes. I cannot leave after coming this far," Aarav pleads.

"You have no idea how dangerous this can get. I do not want any excuses. It's an order."

There is silence on the other end for a while. Then Aarav announces," Sir, you remember that pen you gave me. I think it is time to use it."

The line went dead.

VII-2020

The girls' dormitory

A dazzling ray of sunlight enters the girls' hostel wing. There is chatter of excited girls in the common hallway. Roshini is brushing her teeth while reminiscing about last night's dinner. Asha seems to be waking up from a fever dream while Shaina is dressed up and ready to complete her biology assignment.

"Has anyone seen Jannat?" Roshini says after spitting out the white soapy toothpaste. A rim of snowy foam around her mouth.

"The bee went to look out for some fresh morning nectar, I guess," Shaina chuckles proudly at her joke.

"Metaphorically correct," a panting Jannat wearing blue tracksuit growls.

"Wow, I would never have the motivation to do that, ever," Asha sloppily chimes while stretching her hands so wide she could hug three elephants at once.

"Woah! You have the handspan of a hawk," says Roshini.

"We need to have this secret animal name for everybody," Jannat winks while undoing her shoelaces.

"We will think about that at breakfast. Let's go," barges Shaina trying to hurry the girls.

"Wait, where are my shoes?" Asha screams while letting go of her soft toys.

The Green Lawn Dining hall is massive. The roof has gargoyles and intricate carvings, while the walls have paintings and quotes from the wisest philosophers. No sooner does Roshini step into the hall than she begins scrunching her nose. She gets the deep flavours rooted in her brain and the synapses looking for the last time she had those flavours.

They settle down with their trays, all teeming with delicious gastronomical delights.

"You were talking about the name-giving ceremony. Let us do that," says Roshini biting into a strawberry.

"You love food. You could be an American Pygmy Shrew. They eat three times their body weight daily," Shaina adds while going full geek mode and adjusting her glasses.

"That does not quite ring. Think of something else," Asha pouts while squinting her eyes, trying hard to think.

"Have you guys tried this new waffle?" Says Ahmed while joining them with a tray full of the most colourful delights.

"Heard about the hiking trip next week?" Roshini jumps in.

"Ohh, yes! Excited as always," says Ahmed while dipping his waffles into three equally vibrant sauces.

"One week seems long. I cannot wait to visit downtown Darjeeling," Jannat mesmerises.

"If that's the case, we can break some rules, potentially some bones too," Ahmed sneers.

"What do you mean?" Asha ducks in with interest.

"The gatekeeper takes an acute break around 8:15 pm. We can sneak out of the back entrance and come back around 10:30 pm ," Ahmed jumps.

"Or get caught and serve detention," Shaina snaps back.

"When was the last time you had fun?" Roshini wailed.

"Everybody in?" Ahmed looks around. Jannat nods, Asha does double thumbs-up. Roshini cheers, and Shaina does a double eye roll before finally saying yes.

"Meet me at the old storeroom at 8 pm. Wear a dark hoodie and think of a scam story if we get caught," Ahmed chunks in the last of his waffles after mopping the cream and raspberry coolie.

VIII-2020

The girls' dormitory, same evening

Jannat scans the room. As no one is in sight, she shoots for her runaway bag. She keeps shuffling the items until her eyes land on the black metal device.

She picks it up and calls her emergency number.

"Hello, Bluewhale. Bees will buzz the city after the sun goes down," Jannat whispers.

"A lot of rodents have been dying these days. Hope the bees meet them," Bluewhale hisses.

"They will," Jannat hangs up.

IX-2020

The backside hall, 8 pm

Ahmed raises his binoculars tc check on the gatekeeper. Roshini, Jannat and Asha calculate the risk of jumping from that height. Shaina is sweating but reluctant to leave them.

"What if we don't make it in time?" Shaina nervously asks.

"We blame it on you, simple," Roshini squawks.

One hundred metres ahead, the gatekeeper yawns. The gatekeeper gets up and starts walking in the other direction. As soon as Ahmed gives a signal, Roshini jumps.

She makes it through with a slight thud on the landing.

"That was easy!" She exclaims while checking her arms and legs with gleaming eyes.

Ahmed follows with similar aercdynamic descent. Jannat goes next, landing smoothly and giving everyone a thumbs-up.

Asha pats Shaina's back and says, "Go for it."

"What if I fall?" Shaina hisses back.

"Oh, but my darling, what if you fly?"Asha dreamily singsongs.

"Falling is not the worst-case scenario. Three weeks in the hospital wing is more enjoyable than you think," Roshini mutters, stone-cold.

Everyone below starts cackling.

"Enough of your mockery. I am going to jump. Countdown, please," orders Shaina.

"3,2,1, and jump," Ahmed cheers.

Shaina lands clumsily on the ground while Asha quickly fills the vacant spot behind her. She hands Ahmed the Binoculars. All of them circle and take an oath.

Ahmed commences, "If we get caught."

"Blame it on Shaina!" The others cheer.

Shaina rolls her eyes and mouths, "Not funny".

They flow with the wind and go towards the city.

Same Day. 9 pm

"Don't you guys wanna try Thukpa?" Asha requests.

"Of course. Which place should we go to?" Jannat chimes.

"The store around the corner has the best momos and thukpa. It has been around for more than twenty years," Roshini claims.

"Wow, but they cannot beat Shaina. She has been around longer than the dinosaurs, watching humans evolve and dwell in their stupidity. Where do you think all the grumpiness comes from?" Ahmed frowns, impersonating Shaina.

All of them cackle into synchronous laughter, cruising the streets of Darjeeling.

They get seated in the warm and cosy chairs in Salima Momo Palace. An older woman with greying hair greets them and takes their order.

Roshini introduces her, "This is Nandini Aunty. She owns most of the momo places down the street.

Feeding delicious food to hungry mortals since 1997."

"Stop Praising me. It won't earn you a discount," Mrs Shah giggles.

"You brought a new friend this time. Hello, I am Nandini Shah. Glad to see you here."

"Nice to meet you, Nandini Aunty. I am Jannat Resoulda, and I joined their school a few days ago," Jannat politely adds.

Nandini nods and gets back to their order.

The entire store steams with the warm and comforting smell of Thukpa, a flavorful broth simmered with chicken and spices. The steam from freshly made momos erupts from the mucktoo. Jannat lets herself drown in the mesmerising aroma surrounding her.

Roshini gets up from her seat, and returns with a cute white and grey spotted cat in her arms. She sits down and says, "Meet my old friend, Sammy. He is devilishly cute and attention-seeking," she adds while stroking Sammy.

Jannat pets Sammy while Nandini Aunty returns with their order.

Their food arrives, and Roshini's eyes widen like the Gollum from Hobbit. In a parallel Universe, she might be the Gollum stuck in a food paradise with a ring that subtracts her calories.

After taking their first bite, they erupt with satisfaction and continue eating for a while.

Nandini Aunty smiles at them with generosity. She feeds Sammy and adds, "A lot of rats have been dying lately. I wonder if Sammy has enough food?"

The workers sigh and continue their preparations. Nandini Aunty turns back and smiles at Jannat; that smile implies more than hospitality, meant to threaten and instruct simultaneously.

Jannat returns the smile.

Her watch strikes 9:20. She slurps her noodles, thinking of meeting the rodents.

XI-2010

Date 30th August 2010 By Suchita Verma

Gun Shots heard at Local Inn near Ganeshgram

Around 10:00 pm, near the Sahay Inn in Ganeshgram, Darjeeling, several gunshots were heard by the residents. The owner of the inn, Mahesh Shah, has been called in for investigation by the police. Tonga drivers reported people escaping from the inn a while after the shots were fired.

The public is terrified after yesterdays incident. The police are thoroughly investigating the case and plan to involve more forensic research.

The people staying at the inn that night were tourists from cities like Mumbai, Shimla and Delhi.

Sahay Inn, Ganeshgram

Research is being done into their backgrounds and, some of them are held in custody.

Till now, no names or statement has been released by the authorities. We hope that the police can catch the miscreants as soon as possible.

Ten years ago:

Reporter: Suchita Verma

Date: 31st August 2010.

Around 10:00 pm, near the Sahay Inn in Ganeshgram, several gunshots were heard by the residents. The Inn's owner, Mukesh Shah, has been called in for investigation by the police. Tonga drivers reported people escaping from the Inn a while after the shots were fired.

The public is terrified after yesterday's incident. The police are investigating the case and plan to involve more forensic research.

The people staying at the Inn that night were tourists from cities like Mumbai, Shimla and Delhi. Research is being done into their backgrounds; some are held in custody.

Till now, no names or statement has been released by the authorities. We hope the police can catch the miscreants as soon as possible.

XII-2020

Downtown Darjeeling

Roshini and Jannat hop to the shops with souvenirs and ramble from one place to another.

The rest are gleefully walking around, looking at the view. Asha gets her camera, capturing a few shots of her friends under the shop lights. Ahmed smiles gleefully while Shaina tries to adjust her glasses.

“Wait, I wasn’t done yet,” Shaina complains after placing her glasses in her pocket.

Asha giggles and says, “It was candid. Sometimes, the moment is ready while you are still preparing to live it.”

“Now, whose insta caption was that?” Ahmed mockingly adds from behind.

“Sometimes, I think, and that was an utterance from my experience,” Asha snaps back while moving her head around and laughing childishly.

"Well, good to know that somebody else also has thoughts apart from me," Shaina adds with an eye-roll and continues to laugh with them.

Asha adjusts the saturation on her pictures and shows them to the other two.

"I look older with the glasses, don't I?" Shaina chimes in, squinting to absorb most of the picture.

"I mean, long before the dinosaurs lived is pretty old, isn't it?" Ahmed snarkily mutters while snickering from behind.

"Enough of your bickering around. Does anyone want to go towards the hilly part? I want some shots of the night-lit city market," Asha chirps.

All five sway and move until they reach the city's quieter side. Here, they can listen to the mellow chirping of the cuckoo and shallow whispers of the trees. Shaina stops and inhales the beauty caressing her senses. She is finally at peace and enjoying herself for the first time since they left.

Asha starts moving around to find the best angle and lighting. Jannat stands beside her, completely mesmerised by the charm of the city.

Ahmed is absentmindedly kicking stones and wandering about the place.

He kicks one which reaches Roshini's feet, and they start kicking it back and forth like a football, wholly immersed in their sporting adventure.

Shaina walks closer to a tree and starts observing it closely.

Asha finds a nice spot but stumbles a little while taking her snap. Luckily Jannat holds her down, bringing her back to an upright position.

"Dude, I almost fell down the hill," Asha sighs with relief.

Jannat faintly says, "Oh, but my darling, what if you flew?"

"You sticketh my own dagger in me?" Asha says with her hands on her hips, flabbergasted at Jannat's wit.

Ahmed spots Shaina and shouts, "Hey Shaina, if you are done carbon-dating the tree, we are nearing our time limit."

Shaina turns to shoot back at Ahmed but stops mid-sentence and what leaves her throat is a wail turning into a scream as she sees what happens before her.

Ahmed gets a mighty blow on his left cheek, which knocks him down. Shaina rushes to help Ahmed. Asha and Jannat make their way through the terrain, quickly pacing the distance.

"This foolish guy is the reason I got punished," jitters Raghav cracking his knuckles after hitting Ahmed.

The fight continues. Ahmed boxes Raghav's ear, followed by a harsh nudge on his knees.

Raghav tries blocking the slams but stands unsuccessful.

Asha and Roshini try blocking the two but are reduced to meek bystanders. Raghav hits Ahmed for the second time on his cheek, his punch traversing its way down Ahmed's neck and knocking him down. The impulse of the movements sends shivers down everyone's spine.

Shaina and Roshini come running to save Ahmed.

They try waking him up by tapping his face and calling his name.

Asha opens her bottle and sprinkles water over his face.

They hear a loud thud on the ground. Jannat watches Raghav demolish below her kick.

"Is Ahmed okay?" She asks with a concerned tone.

"Yeah, he is fine. No potential bone breakage as foreshadowed," Shaina mutters.

"We should get going before this Raghav guy puts out more of his fight sequences," Jannat stares at the wailing guy next to her, wondering how long before he gets up. She recalled the last time she had kicked someone, the guy who had bullied her younger sister.

Shrishti. She remembered her reflexes at that distinct moment. The months of training swept the guy to the ground without a breath or shudder.

She was dangerous, which she needed to be.

"But why did he fight in the first place?" Asha complains.

"Ahmed will let us know when he is conscious. Let us move now," Roshini says with a tight-lipped smile.

Asha and Roshini carry Ahmed, who gets up from his temporary sleep.

Shaina bends down to retrieve Ahmed's bag, not noticing a few things fallen behind during the chaos.

Jannat waits for the others to clear out and silently retrieves the dead rat she had secured beneath the rocky terrain. She hastens while counting under her breath.

As she runs to reach her friends, she turns to find Raghav slowly coming back to life, picking up his trodden belongings from the rocky paths.

She stops counting. Raghav sustained the concussion for three minutes and thirty-six seconds, a lifetime more than the last guy she had kicked.

XIII-2020

On the same day at the girl's hostel room

"Ahmed was promoted to Captain of the football team last week as Raghav had been suspended due to his poor performance," Roshini mutters while gasping for air.

"Raghav lost his position among his friends and started developing this grudge against Ahmed, whose repercussions we saw earlier today," Asha continues.

Jannat nods in agreement while Shaina stares at the stars absentmindedly.

"That kick was so precise, Jannat. How did you do it?" Shaina asks, still staring at the window.

"As I told you earlier, my training," Jannat adds with a weak half-smile.

"Seems like they trained you well," says Shaina, now gaping straight at Jannat.

Jannat's insides shiver with fear She needs to be more cautious with Shaina around.

The girls slowly drift to sleep while the night entrenches the leaden sky.

Jannat slowly gets up from her bed, tucking in her pillows to add some volume. She dives for her runaway bag and moves to the washroom. Turning on the light, she takes out her torch, a fresnel lens, a penknife, a glass and a notepad.

She closes the curtains and places the torch on the windowsill. She flicks it on and retrieves the dead mammal. Slicing the stitches, she removes a black box from its belly, opening the box to gain a stamp. The stamp has a tiny dot behind it. Filling the glass with an inch of water, she carefully places the stamp in it. A minute black film escapes on the water surface. She punches her lens into cardboard, putting the dot on the lens with her finger.

This part was crucial; if she dropped the black dot, she could spend years searching the floor and would never find it.

She adjusts the lens in front of the torch till she can read the microdot.

Reading her microdot, she notes down the encrypted text on her notepad.

Fifteen minutes later, she has a code on eight by eleven inches of paper, all encrypted and safeguarded.

"Enough for today," she whispers to herself.

XIV-2020

Green Lawn Central School

"Good Morning, students, meet your new House In-charge, Mr Somprakash Sinha," Mrs Sharma welcomes a fierce-looking gentleman, holding a pair of binoculars. His strides echo in the still room. He walks with an explicit purpose and a sense of belonging.

His sharp eyes intently scan the crowd. He clears his throat and adds, "Thank you, Mrs Sharma. Nice to meet you all. I am Somprakash Sinha, your new House-In-Charge. Mr Singh had to resign due to pressing family issues. I intently take this job. If you ever notice something peculiar or strange, inform the department immediately. Remember, together, we thrive."

He clapped his hands and stepped backwards, nodding politely at Mrs Sharma. She forwarded the gesture and continued with her class.

Lunch Break:

"Why was Mr Sinha carrying binoculars, though?" Roshini curiously asked Asha.

"Might be his fashion sense, didn't you see those fancy pants? He seems like someone who would understand Modern Art," Asha reasons out.

"He did seem slightly intimidating, though," Jannat hisses.

"Well, only if you have something to hide," Shaina snaps back.

"Enough with your mind games, Shaina. Jannat saved me yesterday. Can you stop keeping tabs on people for a day?" Ahmed adds in a pleading tone.

Shaina stares at him in silence. Jannat swallows and looks sideways to avoid their gaze.

"Hey Ahmed, everything okay with your health?" Roshini asks compassionately.

"I am fine, just that I can't find my locket," Ahmed says with a shrug, brushing the place around his neck where the piece of metal belonged forever.

"A few more of my things are missing," he adds with a disheartened face.

"I picked up your things. Maybe I left something behind. Sorry about that, Ahmed," Shaina chirps.

"You guys rescued me yesterday. I will forever be grateful for that," Ahmed's eyes gleam with a kind tinge.

"Ahh...well!We might want free momos in that case," Roshini chuckles.

"Sure thing!" Ahmed says, standing upright. "Next official school trip, my treat."

The bell rings, and they rush to their classroom.

Mrs Sharma resumes teaching, "Who will tell me about lethal substances now?"

Shaina shoots up her hand. On Mrs Sharma's call, she answers, "Cyanides and arsenic are some of the most powerful poisonous substances known to mankind."

"Good, Shaina. Just sniffing a specific cyanide concentration is potent enough to kill you," she remarks.

"How would we figure out what cyanide smells like, then?" Raghav asks from the other corner.

Ahmed's jaw twitches. He tries to look straight and avoid the intruder.

"It smells like bitter almonds to some people, while others detect no scent," Mrs Sharma says nonchalantly.

"How about biting a cyanide pill?" Jannat inquires. "How quickly can that kill someone?"

"A matter of seconds, Jannat," Mrs Sharma replies. "Even less than that, to be precise."

Jannat nods. Her eyes well up with tears. Recalling the first time she heard the word cyanide.

The incident that transformed her life created her new identity.

XV-2010

Safehouse

Aarav's Diary Entry - 24th August 2010.

Bluewhale signalled me through the non-drivers end. I opened the car door and checked that our dog was fast asleep behind us.

We drove out of the Inn, the gatekeeper smiling at us, gently laying his eyes on our pet, whom we often travelled with.

Nearing the check post, we safely landed near the toll booth. The officer asked me some follow-up questions. He handed me some papers back, and I smiled, half-relieved.

Hoping that all our inquiries go the same way, we continued driving.

We arrived at a deserted bypass. I pulled over and shuffled through the papers handed to me. Bluewhale started decrypting them slowly.

He stretched out the codes we obtained earlier and tried to compare his findings. I glanced outside and scanned my surroundings.

Five minutes passed by. Bluewhale glimpsed at me with a worried expression and handed me his discoveries.

I clutch the decrypted text, trying to work out what it hides.

Save the date for the two,

Crumbly, tall the world before me,

I stand here alone, keen and tender,

But my heart beats louder and louder,

Chide! Please let it chime,

No frail illnessstands in the way,

Dtime the journey,

It's odd, I know,

Are you ready to go?

Jerk on the way, my dear,

The element remains fonder,

In we go, up and close,

God's pure gaze will help you cross the way.

I squinted my eyes and tried to think. Suddenly, it hit me. Save the date - I wrote the mentioned date on the paper-

14-10-2010

Crumbly, tall the world before me,
I stand here alone, keen and tender,

Jerk on the way, my dear,   14-10-2010 ←

I number the words and save the two. 1 - Tall, Ta (saved). 4 - keen, ke(saved).

Once I finish with the date, I start saving letters backwards:

I save 0 - Je, 1-el and so on.

Going through the entire scroll, I end up with the sentence-

TakeMychilDtodarJeelinga

On further unfurling, I end up with my message-

Take my child to Darjeeling -A

I step out, clutching the shotgun in my right hand; I open the dog's door and lift him. The fur-clad silhouette ruffles under the pressure of my arm.

I shift it to find the child I will be repositioning tonight. Fast asleep, probably due to some medication. Turning the dog's disguise back on the child, I completely conceal the baby.

I signal Bluewhale to move fast.

XVI-2020

The House-In-Charge office

Mr Somprakash was seated in his office sipping chai while reading the latest developments in the school. He prided himself in always being upfront on facts and stories.

Just as he was about to finish, the serene atmosphere was invaded by the ringing of his cellphone. He did not identify the number, but he picked it up regardless. It might be a pensive parent or another recruiter.

The voice on the other end knocked him out. His eyes emblazoned with fear and grew as large as apricots, his hands got clammy, and his grip on the glass case loosened as he stuttered out a muted response.

He had tried his best to keep his past away, but the further he drifted from it, the closer he got to his fears.

"Boss, is that you?" he managed after a brief pause.

Moments later, his cellphone fell with a thud on the mahogany table, leaving a stub.

A stub that was also left in Somprakash's cerebrum.

The Dining Hall:

"Jannat, are you okay?" Shaina inquired with kind eyes.

"Ahh, yes, I am fine. Why do you ask?" Jannat pleaded.

"You look worried after the cyanide symposium," Shaina explained.

They heard a loud thud from the nearby office.

"Oh my! What was that?" Asha screeched with surprise.

"Seems like Mr Sinha is having a bad first day," Ahmed replied.

"Should we check on him? He might be hurt," Roshini pensively muttered.

"Yeah, let us go," Jannat said, hurriedly taking the cobblestone path to the House-In-Charge's office.

Knocking gently on the teakwood door, Jannat peered into the office.

"Pardon my inquisition, but are you okay, Sir? We heard a noisy thud moments ago," Jannat politely put forward.

"I am just fine, my phone slipped, and this table makes more noise than you would think. All that strong mahogany, isn't it?" he joked with a cheeky smile.

"Yes, mahogany has a very high resistive force," Shaina chimed in.

"Yes, it must. Well, resume your lunch and thank you for stopping by," Mr Sinha resumed reading his papers while the students thumped on the cobblestones again.

Sweat trickled down his brow, which he quickly swung away with his index finger. He handled the intrusion rather well, he thought to himself. Now, time to focus on his mission.

XVII-25TH AUGUST 2010

Somewhere near Ganeshgram, Darjeeling

Aarav's vehicle slowly encountered the Ganeshgram orphanage. An older woman is tending to her plants in the garden. Bluewhale stops the car and examines the place. He alerts Aarav, who stoops low to recover the sleeping baby.

Aarav cradles the baby in his lap, and Bluewhale honks three times. The woman in the garden gets up and places a bamboo woven basket below the tree. She walks towards the main office door.

Opening the car door, Aarav wraps the baby in a blanket. Then stealthily covers the gun in his other hand.

Entering the garden, he positions the baby in the basket, whispering a gentle prayer. He camouflages among the bushes just when Bluewhale reverses the car. The woman arrives again, covering the baby with some fruits she plucked.

She carries the basket inside, humming a folk song.

Aarav climbs the fence behind to join Bluewhale in the car. They rush towards their Inn.

Once they enter the Sahay Inn, Mukesh greets them, and his wife Nandini offers them lunch. They quickly eat as Nandini offers more servings. She smiles warmly and brings out some old papers from her drawer.

"I read the news report about a fire in the Singhania tea refinery that occurred a few weeks ago," Aarav says, holding the article.

Nandini holds in her tears while recalling memories of her son, who supervised the plants and machinery.

Bluewhale comforts and reassures her that they will get to the depth of the matter.

"I bet there is some foul play involved," Mukesh sighs.

Aarav opens his leather case back in their room, holding out his investigation so far.

"The fire seems to have occurred due to explosive substances handled impulsively. But, what could be volatile in a tea refinery? They do not use potent chemicals in there," Aarav says intently.

Bluewhale nods and clasps his report papers.

"I feel that the owners are suppressing something," Bluewhale suggests.

“The plant’s owner, Mr Ram Singhania, died two months ago in an accident. His wife, Ayesha, fleedwith their son immediately after that. I have a hunch that this was an accident,” Aarav concludes.

“Why would his wife run away?” Bluewhale questions him.

“The locals believe it was to protect her son, as he legally owns all the Singhania plantations. Greedy relatives would not waste a second to pounce upon him,” Aarav continues.

The sun stoops lower among the hills as Aarav reads and puts information together. He notes to find out more about the chemicals in the tea refinery.

Just then, there is hurried tapping on their door. Aarav squeezes his shotgun. Meanwhile, Bluewhale holds his weapon behind his back, slowly opening the door.

Mukesh enters, hyperventilating heavily, his forehead teeming with sweat. He closes the door and tells them about a person who came in a bit ago, questioning about two strident men. He informs them that he alerted their friend and they needed to leave immediately.

Bluewhale starts packing while Aarav collects his papers and stuffs them into the leather case. Soon, they manage their wigs and place them over their heads, covering their countenance with more facial hair. They take off their jackets and adjust the wire attached from their waist to their neck; wearing a different shirt, they etch the collar button with the control wire.

They recheck their stuff, remove their tracking and recording devices from their hiding places, and store them in their luggage. They take the secret passageway through the opposite side. They make it safely outside, where a new car awaits them. Inside, Somprakash waits for them, already disguised.

Aarav gets into the backseat lowering himself and opening the compartment that leads to the void beneath the seats. Bluewhale gets into the space, and Aarav closes the compartment again.

Holding his collar button, he signals to Somprakash that they were safely concealed. Somprakash felt a tinge through the metal wire covering his right arm and leading to the receiver he hid near his abdomen. He ignites the engine and swiftly takes to the main road.

Moments later, he senses another twinge around his right arm. He pulls over and waits for a few moments. Then, he pushes his belt buckle to give his friends a safe signal pass. They huddle out of their hiding and whisper gently.

Somprakash takes out his phone, pretending to dial a number.

Aarav informs him about their research and the fires in the tea plant from behind.

Somprakash shakes his head, gesturing that there is nothing he knows about that. He had tried entering the main room to get to know his boss, but he (the boss) kept protecting his identity.

He opens the license drawer and hands them his intel. Aarav stuffs the papers in his leather case. Somprakash nudges his belt buckle while pretending to hang up on his call.

A while later, he resumes driving, sensing a wave through his shirt sleeve.

He continues driving them through the highway, leading them to a densely forested area.

Aarav and Bluewhale move out of their obscuring compartment and thank Somprakash, scurrying to their safe house.

Somprakash parks the blue vehicle in the trees, leaving the keys masked near the compartment. He moves out and walks towards the busier part of the town, mentally planning to track the next bus to Ganeshgram.

XVIII-2020

Green Lawn Library

Jannat sits in the far corner of the library, retrieving her deciphered codes from the night before. She scribbles them on a scroll and starts thinking.

Oh, the mountains utter in pride,

Overlooking the leaves below,

Do we need to take a stride,

To prevent the empire from flow,

Wondering with freshness,

Bubbling and silent,

The wail pot hums with joy,

As encircled with kindness.

Wailing with boredom, she grips her coffee and takes a sip. Looking at her watch, she realises it is time to head back to her dorm. She picks up a classical symbology book, hoping it will help her discover the code.

She thanks the librarian and heads out the hallways. Stepping back on the cobblestone path, she heads over to the girls' dormitory when suddenly she hears some mumbling from the room nearby. Sitting on the opposite seats, she scavenges her pouch to pick out a tear-drop-shaped tiny recorder. She carefully places it on the windowpane, pretending to read her book. Once the mic is set up, she heads out in the evening rays back to her friends, who might be waiting with pillows in hand.

XIX-25TH AUGUST 2010

Somewhere near Ganeshgram

Somprakash gets a seat in the G-24 Purangram bus. Holding out the change for the ticket collector, he gazes out the window. His phone blares, so he fetches it from his pocket and answers the call.

"When will the next parcel be sent?" he hears from the other end.

"Sir, the refinery is busy today. We won't be able to transport the goods. I will ensure that your parcel is given out tomorrow," Somprakash whispers.

"It better be quick, or you will lose your payment," the man on the other end orders.

"Yes, Sir," Somprakash cancels the call.

He pinches his belt buckle and transmits a signal to his friends in the safe house. He nestles himself comfortably and calls his subordinates at the refinery. Ordering them to clear lanes for delivery the next day, he sits calmly, waiting for his stop to arrive.

XX-2010

Safehouse

Aarav empties his communication device box on the counter, looking for a new sim card.

He shuffles the tiny, junk-like mix till he finds a new, unused one. Scavenging the sim card and inserting it into his burner phone, he dials a number etched in the neurons of his brain.

A woman stiffly picks up on the receiving end, "How are you?" She says in a worried but pleased tone.

"I am fine. Is Jannat okay? What about my little one?" he mumbles with sorrow in his voice.

"They are great. Torturing me every day with their burning questions," she jokes.

"How are you, Namita?" he asks.

"I am good, just taking care of the kids and managing my job. Will you be back for our younger one's birthday?" she manages after a brief pause.

"You know how things go. My life is dull for the most part. I have a few seconds to shine and use my skills, but the time it takes for those seconds to arrive is quite long. I will try my best, though. I think I need to go," Aarav says through a tight-lipped smile.

"Be safe. I love you," Namita says with tears welling in her eyes.

"I love you too and my wonderful daughters," he says, grinning from ear to ear, his heart swelling with emotion.

Bluewhale is busy making dinner in the kitchen. Aarav lifts the documents given by Somprakash and analyses them. He even looks at the transcripts of the conversations that Somprakash had with the mysterious boss.

Just then, his arm shivers with a signal received from afar. He instructs Bluewhale to interpret the signal.

Sipping his tea, he reads the transcripts of the recent calls. Most calls include the boss demanding Somprakash transfer some packages throughout the country. He wonders what could be in those packages that Somprakash gets paid such a huge amount for providing them.

Bluewhale returns with the message that Somprakash had sent. "The boss has asked for delivery again tomorrow," Bluewhale utters.

"Do you know where the delivery is headed to?" Aarav bounces back.

"No, but we can find out," Bluewhale snickers.

Aarav opens his receptor and listens to the call log. He edits out the boss' voice and listens to it for a long time, trying to recognise it.

"It better be quick, or you will lose your payment," echoed through his ear-pieces.

He opened his computer and studied the wave pattern of the audio clip. The way the word better was pronounced seemed to be giving off a very confident English speaker's aura. In fact, on further inspection, he even compared it to Hermoine Granger's pronunciation of the word.

His receptors gave way to the conclusion that the guy on the other end had a slight British accent that surfaced when he was agitated.

Bluewhale set dinner on the table and invited Aarav.

Aarav got up to share his new findings with his assistant.

"He might have some foreign education," Bluewhale said cheerily, wondering if they might be close to their goal.

"He sounds like he might be in his late twenties, so we should cross-reference all people who are from Ganeshgram and have spent some time near London in the last 7-8 years. We can narrow down the spectrum that way."

They had dinner with contentment. The parathas tasted splendid after all their adventures throughout the day.

If only they knew what was in store ahead.

XXI-2020

The girls' dormitory

Jannat wobbly prodded on the dorm door. The door opened on its own, and she entered inside, taken aback by the silence she was met with.

"Was it not Saturday today?" She wondered.

She heard footsteps from behind her. She stooped low and forward, firmly holding the pen knife hidden in her socks. Just as she was about to turn back, a bunch of pillows got thrown on her, followed by squealing laughter.

"Got you!" Asha babbled from behind her while Shaina and Roshini continued laughing.

"Oye, did we scare you? You look tense," Shaina empathised after the silence.

Jannat let go of her knife and hugged Shaina tightly. Asha and Roshini follow suit and squeeze into a group hug.

Shaina seems shocked by the sudden gesture but gives into the hug.

Seconds later, Asha gains her fighting spirit and launches into her fighting posture.

"Ladies, get ready to be bashed by the three-time PFA champion. Darjeeling renowned, Ashaaa Shinde," Asha growls while doing a martial arts pose with her pillow.

"Oh! Is she a theatre kid? You guys did not tell me," Jannat exclaims, wriggling her brows.

"Yes, clearly overdosed with WWE smackdown commentary," Roshini whispers in her ear.

They quickly clasp their weapons and jump into position.

"Four girls, one title, let the pillow games begin!" Asha shouts.

Shaina smacks down Asha's pillow and lunges after Roshini. Jannat executes a gracious twirl and baffles Roshini, whose pillow meets the ground soon after. Shaina and Jannat stare at each other and strike themselves with a blow. They regain composure seconds later and go for another clash. Meanwhile, Asha bows down to clear the ground.

"Jannat smacks again with magnificent momentum," Asha comments into her makeshift mic.

Shaina handles the smack with her pillow and goes for another slam before Jannat is ready again.

"With her lightning reflexes, Shaina wins!" Asha hollers throughout their dorm.

Jannat slumps on the ground and starts laughing with an immense glow on her face, a child-like wonder in her eyes. Shaina helps her to an upright position, and all of them start laughing.

They continue smashing pillows into each other for hours. Finally, Asha rips another one, maintaining her streak.

"Principal Mehta will be upset about that," she says laughingly.

Shaina mimicks Principal Mehta by furrowing her brows and straightening her posture.

"You know how expensive these feathers are," Shaina says while gesturing with her hands and curling her lips to enunciate her words.

"This pillow has been bru-tah-lee destroyed, yet again," she says while gently shaking her head to show disappointment.

All the girls erupt with laughter and clasp their stomachs while watching their maniacs.

Jannat wondered, "How simple is life? Why was hers so complicated?"

XXII-27TH AUGUST 2010

Singhania Tea Refineries

Sompraksh sifted through the long alleys filled with hand-picked tea leaves, drying on racks after processing. He traversed to the ageing section and tiptoed to the packaging room.

The conveyer belt overflowed with tiny silver packets that contained some of the finest quality tea. Moving swiftly, the workers manually picked up the suitable flavour bags.

The staff greeted him and continued their job.

He inspected the large cardboard boxes in the warehouse, ready to be dispatched. He strode towards the locker room, opening it and helping Aarav and Bluewhale get into the truck's driver seat. He marked the box C-12X576 with a red star and ordered loading all the boxes in the vehicle.

The workers picked up and dispatched the goods quickly into the carrier. Somprakash signalled the truck to move, and Aarav drove the vehicle.

Aarav and Bluewhalecontinued on the Palghar driveway towards the expressway leading to Sikkim.

Neither of them talked during the trip.

They knew they had been followed by a blue minivan for the past hour.

Driving continuously, they waited at a Dhaba for a quick lunch. They ordered their food while noticing the minivan stop there too.

Aarav tweaked the side of his spectacles to activate the camera and note the car's license plate. He could not see the driver from his position.

Bluewhale caught Aarav's actions and paid the bill, indicating their departure. The minivan started in an instant and kept gaining pace slowly.

Aarav got back in the truck, but Bluewhale quickly slipped in the back and started looking for the box with a red mark.

He hovered over the piles, using his flexibility to turn the boxes and look for signs.

After picking and dropping for some time, his eyes settled on some red splashed across a box.

C-12X576 was printed across its side.

He opened his toolbox and took the penknife to work out the adhesive. Opening the box, he discovered the most minor expected item.

Tons of hay stared back at his face. He dug through the dried grass to find a briefcase engraved with an obscure logo. He found that quite peculiar.

Digging out the case, he detected that it had a biometric lock. He shook his head with regret. He kept looking through the hay for some time and found another briefcase locked similarly.

The vehicle impulsed and paced fast, indicating it was time for Bluewhale to return to the front.

He snapped pictures of the briefcases through the lens attached to his clothing and packed up everything.

He removed his jacket to hide the hay stains and grimes. He stripped some of the faux facial hair and took off his wig. He looked completely different from the Bluewhale thirty- seven seconds ago.

Sifting through the piled-up boxes, he moved to the front end again. He retook his seat and explained the situation to Aarav.

Aarav shook his head as he pulled over into a petrol pump.

They called Somprakash and informed him of the contents inside. Somprakash said that he could not help in any way. He was too afraid to risk his safety anymore.

Agonised and hopeless, Aarav continued driving towards Sikkim.

XXIII-2020

Green Lawn Dining Hall

Shaina shuffled through her psychology book, reading out the syndromes she discovered.

Roshini filled her plate with all the delicious goodies in the pastry aisle, recommending Jannat her favourite desserts.

Asha snapped a photo of her aesthetic-looking plate and started thinking of a caption. Ahmed was busy focusing on what Shaina was reading. She caught him peeking and spread the book so he could read it too.

Jannat took a bite of the praise-worthy cronut, an overhyped cross between a croissant and doughnut and her mind erupted into pleasure. Her eyes rolled back, and she had the funniest expression. It was equal parts surprise and disgust. She regained her senses after Asha slammed her with a few spells directed by her imaginary wand.

"Do we get pastries every Sunday?" she asked, reminiscing the bite she took.

Roshini clinked her glass with her cutlery and gave an affirmative nod. Her mouth was busy unfurling the sweet buttery layers of the cronut. Jannat was surprised Roshini managed cognitive thinking while biting such a masterpiece.

Ahmed cleared his throat and managed to get their attention.

"I have had some trouble sleeping after the downtown fight," Ahmed said softly.

"It's been a couple of days since the incident. You might be facing stress after a sudden unexpected trauma. Talking to someone about it might help," Shaina suggested.

Jannat swallows and stares at Shaina's book. She makes a mental note to go through it.

"I'm not that great at communicating my feelings. I don't think the counsellor is the right move now. Also, we could all get in trouble for this," he reasons.

"All of that is more important than your mental well-being. You should consider Shaina's advice. Also, the counsellor will provide you confidentiality," Asha puts forward.

Ahmed nods in agreement, "I will wait for a few more days," he fist-bumps Shaina, and she smiles genuinely.

"Anybody knows where is Miss Grumpy Dino?" Roshini gets into Shaina's face while pretending to search for someone.

"Hey! I gave her that nickname, don't steal my territory," Ahmed bounces back.

Jannat returns to the pastry aisle, only to find it empty and closed. She beelines the table and folds her hands in front of her, pouting a little.

"Ok, did you two exchange personalities while smashing each other with pillows yesterday," Asha asks with concerned eyes.

Jannat shakes her head and smiles a little.

Roshini secretly puts a plate in front of Jannat.

Jannat squeals with delight and accidentally punches Asha as the cronut smiles back at her from the tiny plate.

"Always take second servings when it comes to Green lawn pastries. Also, a little smuggling from the kitchen isn't a major sin," Roshini says with a perfectly timed wink.

Jannat hugs the cronut with her palm and pulls in Roshini for an embrace. She half-mutters a grateful response right when Asha snaps their picture.

#Cronuttottherescue

XXIV-30TH AUGUST 2010

The Sahay Inn

Mukesh was sitting behind the counter, reviewing their business records last month. Nandini offered him some tea and went ahead to manage her shops.

Two young men entered the Inn and tapped on Mukesh's table, startling him a little.

"Have you noticed anything suspicious in the last week?" One of them said while staring right into Mukesh's eyes.

Mukesh was intimidated at first but cleared his throat and wistfully replied, "Could you please be a little more specific?"

The other man grew impatient and spoke discretely, "Have two mysterious young men boarded your place?"

Mukesh said with conviction this time ahead, "No, I haven't noticed any customers of that sort."

They presented him with a photograph of Aarav dressed like a truck driver and asked if he had seen the guy before.

Mukesh was stunned as he could not make out the familiar face at first, but then he saw the scarring on the neck and was sure that it was Aarav.

"I have not seen him before," Mukesh sternly replied.

Both the men asked Mukesh to keep an eye out for anything out of place. They moved out and drove back in their jeep. Mukesh quickly noted their license plate.

XXV-2020

Green Lawn Library

Jannat adjusted her microscope over the symbol of many Greek Gods. She was very keen to learn about Achilles and the war of Troy. Trailing down the microscope, she traced the sketches provided in the book.

She flipped the page and noticed a couplet written about the sketches provided.

She thought she maybe needed to sketch out the verses she had decoded.

Oh, the mountains utter in pride,

Overlooking the leaves below,

She drew a few mountains in her diary and followed them with leaves below.

Do we need to take a stride,

To prevent the empire from flow,

How does one draw the following lines? She wasn't qualified enough for this. Who could help her with these intricate metaphors?

Tired of scanning the fine lines, she closed the book and rested her head on the table. Quickly, she remembered the events of the morning.

She hurried to the self-help section of the library and began looking at the covers. She had never thought of reading in this genre. She loved historical and literary fiction, even some science fiction novels and occasionally savoured a cosy rom-com. But until today, she never realised that reading non-fiction could help her.

She picked up Atomic Habits, a book she had heard a lot about, and even read a few snippets here and there. But this book did not uncover the problem she was trying to cure.

She picked the books sprawled on mental health issues, but none of them seemed familiar to her. She looked at them for some time before thinking back to her training.

This is not who she was. She wouldn't let a few nightmares prevent her from completing her mission in Green Lawn. She was here for a definite purpose. She returned the books and looked at them before walking to her desk.

She picked up her symbology reference book and continued to her dorm. She still had to finish her math homework and complete her English essay.

Tomorrow, she would resume her research again.

XXVI-30TH AUGUST 2010

The Sahay Inn

Nandini arrived at the Inn with leftovers from her restaurant. She rarely cooked at the Inn as there was always food from the day. Occasionally, she utilised her creative skills and conjured a meal straight before leaving the restaurant.

She hung her keys and found Mukesh tensed on the counter. She set the table with some noodles with hot broth.

"I have a couple of errands to run. I will see you in some time," Nandini said, pulling out her keys and a giant bag.

Mukesh slurped his noodles in delight. The climate had gotten chilly lately, so the comforting soup relaxed him. It reminded him of the soup his mom made when he was younger. They did not live in the Terai region back then. Hence, warm and fermented foods were a big part of their diet. He was grateful to have a caring wife as he had basic culinary skills. Moreover, he never had time to take care of himself with the swarming tourists in his Inn.

Just as he finished his meal, he got a call from Somprakash.

"Hello, did you find out something?" Mukesh yelled into the speaker.

"You realise that I can still hear you if you speak normally," Somprakash said, disoriented from the impulsive decibels, "I have warned Bluewhale and his friend. They told me that the intruders might have bugged your Inn."

"I just got pest control over last week. Haiya, why would they release bugs into my Inn?" Mukesh complained, just like he did when Nandini cooked Karela (bitter gourd).

"Bugged means they must have installed audio receptors or cameras," Somprakash patiently clarifies.

"These people are very dangerous, beta. Be careful with them," Mukesh fumbled through his end.

"Yeah, you too. Take care, Kaka," Somprakash ended the call.

Mukesh picked up his dishes and saw Nandini return with her shopping bag teeming with groceries.

“Our vegetable stock almost got over today,” she said, thudding the fresh produce on her counter. We will have to prepare for more customers as winter approaches,” she said, cross-checking the vegetables in her bag with a list.

“You ate?” She asked, checking off the boxes with her fountain pen.

“Yes, it was splendid. It reminded me of my mother’s soup,” he chuckled.

Nandini nodded with a smile and sat down with her supper. They talked about their business and savings. With her younger son’s death in the tea refinery fire, they had lost a considerable part of themselves. Like many others, they stayed strong and struggled to get justice for the wrong done to their family.

A stretch later, Mukesh stepped out to review his daily records. His assistant brought back the customer reviews and coupons. They calculated their expenditure, intently scanning the rows of entered data.

Swift storms started blowing outside. Nandini quickly shut the windows and locked the main door to secure the place.

Right then, they heard a gunshot from the first storey of the Inn.

Mukesh hurried to the stairs with his assistant, and Nandini dialled the local police station. The visitors grew fearful and started running mindlessly through the floors. Nandini tried to calm them, but they rushed out the main door like an angry mob of bees.

They lost their son, their youth and their reputation.

What else would this older couple have to go through?

XXVII-2020

The girls' dormitory

"How am I supposed to remember all these trigonometric equations?" Asha grumbled deep down in her homework.

"Practice more, instaqueen," Shaina winked from the corner.

Jannat arrived with her laptop in hand. She sat down at her desk and resumed her essay.

"Oh! I almost forgot we had this assignment," Roshini gasped and started mumbling rapid mantras with joined hands.

"Are you trying to extend the deadline by cursing our teacher," Asha chuckled, tapping her pencil on the desk while her head bobbed up and down. Jannat looked up and broke into a peal of loud laughter right then.

"I love how Asha laughs with her whole body," Jannat said, clapping her hands in front of her to mimic Asha.

"I am trying to summon the energy to start my essay," Roshini spoke, opening her notepad.

Shaina stooped over to help Roshini with her essay. Jannat turned to face her screen and tapped the keyboard rhythmically. They continue studying as the sun sets lower and the winds grow frenzied.

The big clock strikes nine, and the periodic ding-dong echoes throughout the school.

"Dinner-time," Roshini shouts, banging her laptop close.

"How is she always so enthusiastic about such a monotonous event?" Shaina says with a sophisticated tone.

"It is the simple things in life that matter," Jannat mutters sheepishly to herself as the girls buzz out.

XXVIII-2020

The Dining hall

"Did you hear that the new House-In-Charge almost had a concussion?" two girls whispered as the Four roommates sped up the hallway,

"Didn't he see it coming with those binoculars?" They laughed mockingly.

Shaina sped past them, throwing a judgemental glance that shut them up.

Ahmed sat picking at his stew, separating the chillies from the broth.

Jannat sat beside him with her tray, "Are you okay?" She said calmly.

"Yeah, feeling better after speaking to you all. Shaina suggested I write in my diary, which has greatly benefited me. Pero estos chiles son muypicantes," he joked, fishing the chillies out.

"Ah si, tienes razon," Jannat nods, understanding.

'You guys speak Spanish too?" Shaina jumps in excitement, almost knocking her tray over Roshini.

The three Spanish learners pour out their wisdom and chatter uncontrollably.

Roshini and Asha eye them with curiosity, guessing what they are saying.

The big clock dings again when the students prepare for bed. Jannat slams into her soft pillow and sighs with pleasure at its cosiness.

XXIX-31ST AUGUST 2010

Safehouse

Bluewhale knocked on Aarav's door, equipped with their suspect list.

"Aarav, is everything okay?" Bluewhale sounded concerned.

He waited a couple more seconds before bursting through the door.

He saw Aarav devastated, raking his fingers, almost pulling out his hair. He had never seen his senior crumble past him. He could not imagine what news could make him shudder like this.

Aarav shuffled the paper for Bluewhale to read. Bluewhale caught sight of the Sahay Inn, and his heart fluttered. On reading the rest, he felt so sorry for the old couple. He was so grateful for their hospitality and care. He couldn't imagine what they were going through at the moment.

"My job always hurts people," Aarav said, raising his head slowly to reveal his wry expression. His eyes were glistening with tears as he spoke.

"Bluewhale, you need to leave this place as soon as possible," Aarav turned his head to the side and looked right into his partner's eye, "we cannot waste a second."

"I am not leaving. We came on this mission together. We leave together," Bluewhale replied with a jolt.

"I don't want more people to get hurt," Aarav pleadingly said.

"What if you get hurt? Your family needs you. I have no family," Bluewhale replied.

"Who said you don't have a family?" Aarav hugged Bluewhale. "You must leave Bluewhale, take the locked briefcase, and save my research on a microdot. Inform our seniors about the progress. I will request reinforcement. Consider it an order."

Aarav stiffened a little, pulling out of the hug.

"That poor couple was just trying to help us. Look what happened!" Aarav explained.

"What are you going to do here?" Bluewhale asked.

"I will finish what I started," Aarav confirmed.

They took one last look at each other before parting ways.

Would they ever meet again?

Only time would tell.

XXX-2020

Green Lawn Central School

"Can we talk about what happened the other day?" Shaina cornered Jannat as they were climbing up the stairs after dinner.

"What do you mean?" Jannat furrowed her brows in confusion.

"About you getting tensed up after the pillow-fight scare," Shaina offered.

"No, that was nothing," Jannat averted her eyes and climbed faster.

"If you don't want to talk about it, that's fine," Shaina followed and raced her. But remember, "I am there to listen."

Jannat stopped abruptly and almost teared up. No one had ever said those words to her. She ran away from Shaina and stopped only when she arrived at their dorm. Covering herself with a duvet, she remembered her oath. She reminded herself that she had to do this for her family.

She thought about the code and continued thinking about her research. She thought of calling Bluewhale and asking for help. Still, it would be too risky, with Shaina observing and reading her body language.

The others jostled into their beds.

Jannat stayed still and made no sounds. Her training had prepared her well for moments like these. She didn't realise when she drifted off to sleep.

Jannat felt clusters of light fall on her blanket as she opened her eyes, the incidents of last night falling back to her. She saw the sun illuminated in the sky, gently soaring above the darkness. She checked the clock to find out it was five at dawn. Hoping into her shoes, she gently crept on the floor, animatedly closing the door behind her. In five minutes, she was jogging at her full pace, trying to process the events that had taken place.

Jogging always cleared her mind and steered her focus. It was just her, the wind and her hamstrings shoving her momentum to guide herself forward.

She was taught how to kill people with a safety pin or piece of aluminium foil during training. She was taught how to clear murder scenes and analyse bloodstain patterns to determine the angle of the bullet.

She was never taught how to react to being loved and cared for. She wasn't credited and accounted for her feelings. She was treated as an asset to society, not a human with emotions and thoughts.

But she had known this long before entering this field. It was etched in her oath that she had to put people first, then why was she losing herself with these new people around? Why was she not manipulating them to reveal the information her seniors wanted?

Why was she not following what her father had done?

She stopped mid-run and inhaled ferociously. The memory of her father left a sudden pang in her chest. It was this memory that had given her those nightmares.

She gripped her knees, bent towards the ground, and promised toruncorrectly this time.

XXXI-1ST SEPTEMBER 2010

Ganeshgram

The forensic team has revealed its progress; the bullets seemed to have missed their targets. They were shot from afar, and the skill demanded suggested that a professional had been responsible for the event.

On recognising the terrain that covered the Inn, the officials reckoned that the suspect might have had a hiding spot, which was diametrically opposite the Sahay Inn. They questioned a few locals in the area to reach a better conclusion.

Shyamlal, the tea vendor, said that he had seen Nandini collect a bunch of groceries that night. He also mentioned the storm and the unmistakable sounds of the shots.

Savita, the farm owner, confirmed that Nandini had picked up a bunch of produce. She even utilised the opportunity to market her vegetables.

On further questioning, she revealed that two stern-young men had come investigating combatively a couple of days ago. She didn't recollect their names but did an exceptional job explaining their appearance and car.

Narangi, the barber, had cut the former mentioned men's hair and given them a massage for free on being threatened. He offered their names and other details.

Mukesh was scared about whether to mention the two men or not. Nandini reassured him by telling him to speak the truth. Moreover, they would hurt themselves by trying to hide anything.

He offered the car's license plate number and shared his experience with the two men. Officer Prakash seemed content with his answers and left to investigate further.

Since the shooting incident, no one had approached the Inn. The business had declined rapidly, and the visitors at Ganeshgram further reduced after the incident.

Nandini worked overtime at her restaurants to keep the family running. Mukesh offered to help her at the restaurant, but she asked him to focus on his health.

Somprakash was nowhere to be found, his number had stopped working, and they rarely saw him near the city market.

Mukesh considered visiting Somprakash at the refinery, but Nandini advised him against it.

Officer Prakash returned a few days later with good news. The miscreants behind the shootings had been identified. He did not reveal any more information for legal confidentiality but assured the couple that they would receive justice soon.

Nandini gave him a tight-lipped smile, remembering clearly the last time he had offered the same suggestion.

"The deceased's families will receive compensation," Officer Prakash had announced a week after the Tea Refinery fire accident.

There was no compensation.

She saw him drive back in his jeep before cursing him profusely in her native dialect.

XXXII-2020

The girls' dormitory

Jannat was met with the girls clanking and storming around the dorm when she returned from her run. Asha held Jannat's shoulders dramatically, "We almost forgot that our hiking trip is today."

She screamed while shaking Jannat avidly and burning some of her ear receptors.

"This is your first official outing. We have to do this right," Roshini stammered while simultaneously packing her hiking shoes and closing the washroom door with her foot.

Shaina ushered Jannat to the shower and closed the door behind her. She ordered through the closed door, "You have seven minutes, go fast or stay in the dorm."

The girls struggled to get dressed and packed around their already shabby interiors. Additionally, Principal Mehta blared the halls with reminders of the day's events.

"He has the worst timing," Asha muttered under her breath, holding her ponytail and looking around for a hair tie.

Mrs Sharma took charge of blaring instructions, and the teens dashed as they imagined her stares scanning them like laser guns if they were late.

"We leave for the tea gardens at six-thirty," Mrs Sharma said through her mic, roaming down the corridors and navigating the lost teenagers. Tilting her head to the side, she muttered, "we need to get rid of this hideous gramophone-looking mic."

"I took that personally, Mrs Sharma," Principal Mehta said from behind her when she realised that she had been speaking directly into the audio device.

Mrs Sharma was caught off-guard and laughed nervously, trying to avoid the situation's awkwardness.

The girls burst into laughter, imagining Mrs Sharma's expression at her tiny mishap.

They lined up and rechecked their bags and bones, confirming if they had missed or broken something. They followed out to find Mrs Sharma in her hiking outfit, an emerald-green blouse with robin egg's blue denim jeans and a straw hat. They seldom saw her in casual outfits, but she looked like she could have been a fashionista twenty years ago.

Shaina tilted towards Asha and snarkily added, "I hope you are taking notes. This content could spice up your feed."

Asha nodded and stared at Mrs Sharma in awe. This was going to be her in another twenty years. Mrs Sharma tapped Asha's collarbone with the microphone and asked her to keep moving. Asha bowed down in respect and continued walking.

"Asha looks like she has been hypnotised," Jannat cackled, holding the handrail.

They continued stifling through the stairs and stood in the hallway, buzzing with excited pupils, lined up in rows.

Principal Mehta stood near the stage and gave orders to the staff, while Mrs Sharma hurried with the rest of the latecomers.

After the children settled a bit, Principal Mehta spoke into the mic set up at the podium.

"Today, Green Lawners will visit the Aarey Tea Plantations, and the ninth graders will go hiking and sightseeing later. I hope my students have prepared well for the trip and had a good night's rest. Discipline is a must throughout the outing, but ensure that you enjoy yourselves and learn something new. Each group will prepare and submit a report on the trip the same day, next week."

The last line was met with a disappointing wail passing throughout the crowd of the students. The teachers carried their groups to their respective buses and seated their students, taking attendance soon after. The buses took off one after another, and the kids yelled and rejoiced as they sped out of the entrance.

Jannat took in the wrinkly valleys and green ridges lining the cities. She had sneaked out of the building at night and never witnessed these creations of mother nature. She had to admit that Nature was the most beautiful thing on earth, and Math was the second. Shaina pointed out the tea plantations they were about to visit, speaking rapidly about their history and legacy. Jannat knew they were going to ace that report. The younger students gazed at Shaina with awe as she adjusted her collar and continued speaking.

Asha took pictures of the scenery, and Shaina was busy locating her emergency snack items.

"Why don't you children play something?" Mrs Sharma cheered from the front seat while Mr Somprakash scowled next to her.

The children quickly made teams for a game of Antakshri. It is a game where teams take turns singing a verse from a song, and the other team has to sing a song which starts with the ending letter of the former song.

Asha's team began by singing an old hit Bollywood classic. Asha took the opportunity to enunciate every expression and fulfil her cosplay desires. She vividly danced to the beats and ordered the next team to sing with the letter 'h'.

They burst into a romantic song from a couple of years ago, "Tum hi ho", and the whole bus stopped to let the melodious tunes calm their souls.

They went back and forth and sang all kinds of songs, from new rap songs to older 70's music, to rock and roll and romantic, soulful hits.

The bus halted near a famous breakfast spot, and Mr Somprakash passed boxes filled with sandwiches and juice for the kids to relish.

"Too bad they don't have cronuts." Shaina teased Jannat as she bit her sandwich, the sides of her lips painted with mayo.

Jannat laughed through a mouthful of bread and condiments when Asha jumped in and declared, "that punch you offered after discovering cronuts still hurts. It is good that I did not get a bruise. All my pictures would have been ruined."

"A good cronut is worth the punch," Ahmed said, joining the conversation.

"Perhaps, you should have gotten more the other day," Raghav sneered from the backseat.

"Hey, you backseat bulldog, don't you remember the kicks you got?" Asha snapped back without missing a beat.

Jannat turned her neck and raised an eyebrow at Raghav. He backed down after she held her smoulder like the Rock in Jumanji.

Influential people didn't raise their voices. They just raised their eyebrow.

"That ought to shut him for the rest of the trip," Jannat winked.

They mumbled songs and joked for the rest of the bus journey. The vehicle screeched to a stop near the Aarey Tea Plantations. Mrs Sharma discussed the ticket details and counted the children as they stepped through the iron-clad door.

"Thirty-six, thirty-seven. Where's your tie, Suman?" Mrs Sharma said, quarrelling through her papers.

"She has lasers built in that hat, it seems," Shaina said, widening her eyes with surprise.

"Asha, submit your phone in the bin there," Mrs Sharma pointed to the yellow plastic tray on her left. Asha hesitated but placed the metal covered with her favourite anime character in the tray. Roshini patted Asha on the back to console her.

"Forty-five, forty-six, Roshini, what's wrong with your shoelace?" Mrs Sharma looked down.

Roshini had intertwined her laces around her ankles like the spiderwebs that Tom Holland threw around. It was a wonder how she had not fallen head-first when she walked around.

"It's a part of my look, ma'am. I was going for the totally-forgot-the-trip-chaotic-morning-look," Roshini deadpanned.

"Well, in that case, don't fall down the terrain. You will smell like tea for days," Mrs Sharma said, giving her the cardstock wristband.

Jannat stepped inside the tea colony, fitting the band on her left hand. She was shell-shocked when she saw the sight that waited for her arrival. She gasped in awe, and her eyes and mouth gaped open with curiosity. Mother Nature left no limits when it came to enunciating her beauty. Asha made clicking sounds pretending to click a picture of her flabbergasted friend with an animated expression. Jannat waved her off, giggling in embarrassment.

Shaina felt the ground beneath her and bent lower to gaze at the leaves carefully. "Camellia Senensis,"she said, running her thumb over the dew-laden leaf.

"The only Camilla I know is Camilla Cabello," Asha said, rolling back her torso to let out a laugh.

"Sí, señorita," Shaina said, twirling in a curtsy.

They burst into resounding laughter and continued walking through the muddy path.

On the turning ahead, they met the tour guide, a tall, muscular, overly-enthusiastic young man. He looked like the people on National Geographic, only with tanned skin.

"Hi, I am Rohan Shah, your guide for the day. Are you excited?" he cheered loudly as soon as the kids had gathered around him.

"Someone drank too much coffee," Asha whispered.

The younger children yelped a loud affirmative response. Somprakash stuffed himself between the children listening patiently.

"We are going to learn the tea culture of Darjeeling today," Rohan said, smiling widely.

"This experience will truly move you," Rohan continued, waving his hands in front of him like a choir director.

"Another theatre kid," Jannat said in recognition, "today is going to be a long day," she said, sighing with amusement.

They were divided into groups of four, consisting of a leader each. Shaina was their group leader. She made sure they walked carefully through the rocky path. After stumbling, pebble-kicking, frowning because of spidey-aesthetic-laces-muddy-now and visual scanning of the foliage, they reached the plantations.

The tea leaves were scattered as far and wide as they could see. They saw tiny ladies with bamboo baskets picking at the tender nodes with care and expertise. Rohan looked pleased with the reaction he received.

"The Aarey Plantations are stretched to cover an area of 50 acres, making it the largest tea plantation in Darjeeling. We employ over 20,000 locals and produce 15 per cent of the total tea consumed in India. More than 60 per cent of our employees are trained women," Rohan said, beaming proudly.

"My mother has also been a part of Aarey for over 30 years," he said, waving to the woman standing far in the corner.

"That's how I became interested in tea and brewing. Let's keep moving, children," he declared loudly, stepping down from the boulder.

They moved into the plantations, surrounded on all four sides with floral aromas and an abundance of chlorophyll. Asha stopped mid-way and turned around, lowering her head with closed eyes and breathing in the tranquil air that wound her.

"Shakespeare left his heroine in Darjeeling," Shaina said, wobbling and manoeuvring around Asha.

"Mr William, good morrow?" Roshini screamed above the sky, "It seems you left a fellow mortal on Midgard. We request thee to carry thou property. I hath a temptation for the taste of heaven food if you are allowed to carry it with thee."

"What is wrong with you girls?" Mrs Sharma shouted from behind the queue.

Asha seemed to have awakened from her scene reading and ran as fast as she could, Roshini pacing behind her. They giggled as they met Shaina, who had been chatting with Rohan, eyeing the plants intently.

Their literature teacher, Miss Zainab, had been listening to Roshini's monologue. She patted Roshini and asked her to join the drama club if she had the time. Roshini giggled nervously and nodded her head.

"You people must be tired, have some iced tea," Rohan offered.

Trays of an amber liquid filled in cups were passed around. The outsides of the cups dripped with condensed drops around them. Roshini sampled the tea in a small zip-lock she had brought. Jannat gulped the sweet and sour liquid, tired after their stroll.

"The British Raj experimented with growing tea in Assam and Darjeeling, it was successful, and here we stand today. Indians have adopted the tea-drinking culture after the colonial rule," Rohan spoke as they enjoyed their beverage.

"Do you like gifts?" He spoke cheerfully to the crowd.

"Yess," they shouted in response.

"We will be giving everyone samples of our Earl Grey Tea," he said, pointing to the boxes in front of him.

"The Singhania refineries refine our tea. This is a new product we have been working on. Top-secret," he whispered with wide eyes.

Roshini jumped in excitement when her shoelaces tugged, she stooped forward, colling into Asha, and they fell through the alley, crashing against rocks and dirt. Jannat acted swiftly and threw her jacket near the valley. She hurried behind Mr Somprakash and others as they followed the two, rolling speedily down the slope. They stopped near the soft velvety fabric of the jacket. Jannat paced behind, making sure they had no significant injuries.

Mr Somprakash helped them climb the hill, and Jannat stuck behind them to prevent further stumbling.

Mrs Sharma clutched their hands to check their bruises, "I told Roshini to take care of her totally-forgot-trip-chaotic-look earlier."

She rushed towards the first-aid kit.

The rest of the teachers followed behind and supervised the other kids.

Mrs Sharma bandaged their wounds after cleaning them with water and antiseptics. She scolded Roshini for not taking care. Shaina and Jannat helped the fallen ones stand and took them to their seats. The rest of the trip went by, with everyone ensuring the girls were okay. Ahmed ducked in from behind and presented two cups filled with the clear amber liquid he had smuggled.

Roshini hawked and drank hers in two gulps, while Asha courteously muttered a grateful response before downing hers.

Shaina shook her head, laughing and taking a picture of the two trodden queens.

"Hey, you remembered my phone!" Asha clutched the metal to her chest, her cheeks returning to life below the musty dirt that covered them.

"Jannat, thank you for sacrificing your beautiful coat," Roshini said with a grateful smile.

"Anything for you guys," Jannat advanced to hug them but offered a fist bump after noticing their muddy camouflage.

"You people need to shower, stat," Shaina said, pointing their gift bags with exclusive tea towards them.

"You people are the best," Asha said with glowy tears filling her eyes.

XXXIII-2ND SEPTEMBER 2010

An old garage in Punjab

Bluewhale sat across from Namita, holding his cup of coffee. He pressed the pile of papers ahead. Namita inhaled deeply, gaining the courage to read the stack in front of her.

Her eyes randomly focused on the word gunshot, and her heart beat fast with fear.

She scanned the page, reading the sentences intently.

"What is this supposed to mean?" She said, staring into Bluewhale's eyes.

"The allies figured out about our involvement, and Aarav sent me back," Bluewhale placed his cup on the table, sending a rippling thump through the garage.

"Is he okay?" she said with a croak.

"He is one of the finest agents we have. He will be okay," Bluewhale said, tilting his gaze towards the papers.

"You sound like you are convincing yourself more than me," she said with slight amusement in her tone.

"I need your help," Bluewhale pleaded.

"I left that job for a reason, but Aarav had different plans with his career," Namita said, sipping her coffee.

"I came back from a mission. The authorities don't know I am actively working on this case, and they won't fund me. There is no other agent I can trust," Bluewhale came clean to Namita.

"Former agent, now civilian," she said, angling her face towards the closed window.

"You think you can walk away from your past that easily? Our field of work only taints lives; it doesn't heal," Bluewhale said bitterly.

"I have two daughters. One of them hasn't seen her father since she was born. I am their only hope, their only family. I did not just walk away from my past. I left it to create a better future," Namita lowered her eyes to hide the plasma filling her lower lashes.

"Do this for Aarav. He is out there fiddling through the maze. This is the only way we can help him," he said calmly.

"You're good at blackmailing, aren't you?" She said, turning sideways to smirk.

"Learnt it from you," he said, smiling back.

"I love my husband too much, and I might have to agree," she said, hiding the pain in her voice, lowering her head again, letting her black curls obscure her expression.

"Do you want to help me? I won't take much of your time. I am willing to babysit if you want," he said calmly.

"Okay, I will help you. Where do we start?" Namita raised her chin to meet his eyes, scanning his face for any change. Her body language reading skills hadn't left her, although she had left her job.

"I have a briefcase with a biometric lock. I want you to figure out a way to open it. It is a custom lock created for this particular case," he said sharply.

"People are getting custom locks made, and we still hide our keys underneath the doormat," she said, chuckling while raising her coffee cup.

Bluewhale clinks his cup with hers, and they smile at each other.

"To Aarav and this crazy job," she said, wiggling her head from side to side.

"To Aarav," Bluewhale replied, downing the coffee.

"What brand did you use? This is delicious," Namita said, eyeing the liquid with curiosity.

"I'll let you know once you introduce me to your children," he shifted through his luggage and plucked out the case, returning to the table with it.

"You stole this from a Star Wars set, don't lie," she said, running her fingers through the silver grained on top of the case.

"A spy has their secrets," he whispered in her ear.

"I need some equipment and intel," she brushed the lock, looking for a mark or symbol.

"There is not only a symbol but also a code on this case," Namita grazed the engraved numbers.

"C-12X576, that was the number of crates we found it in," Bluewhale snapped.

"Did you run it through the database? We might get a lead," asked Namita.

"I did but found nothing. I don't think it is very relevant," Bluewhale said.

"Probably, I will note it down and look through some details, just in case," Namita grasped the papers and bunched them in her handbag. Bluewhale helped her carry the briefcase to the car.

"If you need anything, call me. I will inform you when I get a lead," Namita said, getting into the driver's seat.

She waved a goodbye which Bluewhale reciprocated, smiling as he retraced his path.

XXXIV-2020

The girls' dormitory

Asha groans as she settles into her bed, fixing up her bandages after the shower. Jannat helps Roshini into an upright position as she tries to pick up something from her drawer.

"You guys couldn't visit the refinery because of us," Asha resented.

"Sorry about that," Roshini said, patting Jannat's hand.

"Your safety is more important than brewing tea," Shaina said, looking up from her homework.

"Touché," said Asha trying to move her blanket to cover her exposed ankle. Roshini took out a box from her drawer, carefully opening it.

"That looks like something my grandma would have," Asha jokes, manoeuvring the soft fabric over her feet.

Roshini focuses on the box's contents and carefully places her tiny zip-lock pouch from earlier.

"Oh my God! What are you, a witch?" Asha said, holding out her arms and widening her brows.

"This is my collection. It has all the food that blew my mind," Roshini said, grinning widely. "I want to discover why these dishes taste so good."

"So, has some of it rotten yet?" Shaina says with disgust.

"Oh, come on! I am not that ridiculous. I store miniature models of the dish I design myself," she said, beaming with pride.

"That is so cool, Roshini Sharma - miniature food enthusiast," Jannat says with wonder.

Roshini giggles while Asha finally covers her toes and sighs in relief.

She removes the Tea parchment to reveal a royal blue cardboard box. It had a giant picture of the hills with some foliage at its feet and the 'Singhania Tea' branding.

The pattern behind the Singhania text was faintly hinting at a city skyline. Jannat chuckled at the juxtaposition and flipped the package. She saw the same skyline mimicked on the entire package but in a very tiny size. You could miss it if you just glanced at the box; it would seem like a geometrical design. She was intrigued by what led the marketing team to choose this packaging. She placed it back in the parchment and went to help Shaina with their report.

Shaina was deep down in her research and notes. Jannat cleared her throat.

"Oh, you're here," she said, lowering her laptop screen. Jannat arrived next to her, and she presented her progress so far.

"There have been fires in that refinery?" Jannat exclaimed with shock.

"Yes, back in the summer of 2010, they built the whole east section again," Shaina replied.

"I did not expect that. Why would a refinery be on fire, though? Isn't it odd?" Jannat looked through the articles Shaina had downloaded.

"They say it was an accident. The owners covered all the press around it, so we don't have a lot of articles. But, I agree with you. Fire in a tea refinery seems odd," Shaina remarked.

They continued bickering and working on their report, reviewing articles and covering their activities, including the jack-and-jill-rolling-down-the-hill component.

Roshini trails her eyes towards the pair, suddenly remembering, "You know, I got an invitation to join the drama club."

"No way, Madamoiselle!" Asha beamed with joy.

"I am not considering joining it," Roshini said warily.

"Why?" Asha jumped in.

"I am not made for exaggerating human experiences. It is for you. I love culinary arts,' Roshini returned a gentle smile to Asha.

"I don't have any friends in the club, only mere acquaintances. You being there would highly motivate me," Asha insisted.

"Reconsider Roshini, all those expressions you come up with while eating. I am sure you will find comfort in acting at some point," Shaina reasoned.

"Yeah. Give it a try. You can leave if you don't feel content," Jannat offered.

"Okay, I might try it," Roshini said, blinking slowly.

Asha tried to move out of her bed to hug Roshini, but she realized that her body had not yet recovered from the fall. She waved her arms and made weird noises until Roshini noticed her and did the same again.

"I am sure she will be more than contented," Shaina mumbled in Jannat's ear.

"God, help us deal with two Asha's," Jannat said in return.

"Amen."

They chuckled softly to not interrupt the wireless communication the dramatists had going on with their arm gestures.

XXXV-4TH SEPTEMBER 2010

Safehouse

Aarav printed the word document he had been working on. It was a list with the names of all suspects for the person with the British accent.

He played the clip again on his computer.

"It better be quick, or you will lose your payment," he paused the audio and peeked at his narrowed-down list of suspects.

Seema Rathore

Manish Rathore

Ganesh Shah

Atul Kumar

Avesh Siddiqui

Satish Sharma

Somya Tandon

Karan Singh

He cancelled Seema and Somya, as the person was a male.

Opening his company's database, he entered Manish Rathore. Seventy-six thousand results loaded up in 0.075 seconds.

He filtered his search to show only people from Ganeshgram, Darjeeling. Three hundred fifty results stared back at him. He presented more filters- alive, age restrictions and education qualifications. He narrowed down the list to find two men having quite a lot in common.

Keenly staring at his screen to note differences, he saw a tiny orange tab on one of the results. Clicking on that Manish, he discovered the blue bookmark symbol. He thanked Bluewhale for his great homework and typed in the results of the remaining bookmarked suspects.

"Bluewhale saved me some hours," he said, waiting for his printer to whizz out the remaining details.

Manish Rathore was a resident of G-35, Ganeshgram. He had been born and raised there. Living with his wealthy grandmother, he had married a wise, rich woman and gone on a world tour with her. Aarav could not imagine this lavish, extravagant man behind such a hustling squad. Still, he never judged a book by its cover. Noting the details of Manish's Ganeshgram villa, he decided to visit him.

Next on the list was Ganesh Shah. Unlike the former noble grandson, he had earned a scholarship and worked as a microbiologist in London. Why would such a successful man want to distribute briefcases in tea boxes? Aarav might have to get intel on this man from other sources, but he could still go through his published research papers.

He sifted through his sim card box and found the right one for the job. Dialling a code before the phone number, he pressed the green button with hope. The first ring, second ring, third ring- and the call got rejected.

He sighed furiously and picked up a different card, dialling again. He pressed the button. Ring one, ring two, ring three- and someone picked up.

"Hello," Aarav said gently through his device.

"What do you want?" the woman on the other end croaked. She sounded impatient.

"I need a favour. Find me a microbiologist, name Ganesh Shah, twenty-eight, five-seven, three research papers published, former Ganeshgram resident."

"Call me tomorrow, same time, keep the money coming," the woman on the other end replied and hanged up immediately.

The spies deployed in different parts of the world always came in handy.

He picked up his attire and disguise after having supper. Perhaps, Manish Rathore might have to provide him with some hospitality tomorrow.

XXXVI-2020

Green Lawn Central School

Somprakash held his phone in one hand, switching on the torch. He looked through the school records.

Whatever he was about to do was illegal. He moved around the Principal's office to find the large green hardbound register. The boss had been severe in the call. It had been ten years since he had last heard his voice.

He recalled the old days when he was still working with aromatic tea leaves. He found himself brave to return to the place that had taken so much from him earlier.

Before trespassing the office, he had bypassed a couple of cameras from the security room.

The guard took a stroll for a defined time interval. This offered Somprakash the perfect time window to sneak into the office.

He had seven minutes left to leave the office and reset the cameras. He continued searching through the drawers with the flashlight between his teeth.

He heard a loud thud outside the office, which startled him, sending the flashlight thundering through the drawers. He struggled with his phone, finally placing it in his pocket and heard the door lock creak behind him.

Locking the drawer quickly, he hid between the cupboards. The door swung open, and he heard footsteps clattering inside. He held his breath and tried to peep through the hinges of the closet.

The footsteps came to a stop, and the chair was moved. Through the gap, Somprakash saw Principal Mehta seated on his cushioned chair. Principal Mehta opened a drawer and shuffled some papers. He couldn't see the other person in the room.

Just as Principal Mehta closed the drawers, Somprakash remembered the flashlight he had dropped. Dread filled his chest as he thought of his future if that flashlight was discovered. He prayed in his head, hoping that the Gods would save him this time too.

Principal Mehta plucked out a letter and held it in front of the other person in the room. Somprakash shifted in the tiny space, trying to get a hint of the other person.

"Your mother has sent in these letters. I thought of personally giving them and having a chat," Principal Mehta said, handing out the papers.

"I know it might be hard for you to cope. If you require any support, the school is always there," he smiled softly.

"Thank you, Sir. I have a bunch of friends now, and I like it here," the other person muttered.

Somprakash registered the voice of a female. He stared at his sweaty palms, wondering how he had ended up here.

"Before you leave, did you tear off a couple of pillows?" Principal Mehta said sternly, his posture stoic, the fatherly smile wearing off.

"Umm, I am sorry, Sir, I promise not to vandalize school property again," the girl squeakily replied.

"You better not. Asha can pass on her personality traits," he said, chuckling slightly, wiping his glasses.

"Go, have dinner now," he said just when the clock struck, and a loud clang was heard.

He stepped up from his chair, noting a few more things in his register. He churned a key into one of the ample cupboards, opening it and bringing out a bulky green log. Somprakash strained his eyes to look at the set of keys. It did not seem likely that he would be able to discover what the boss ordered him to.

Principal Mehta added some details to the register and closed it with a loud thud. Opening the drawer again, he placed it inside and locked it safely.

Somprakash waited inside as the lights went out and the door knob whistled. He counted to 100 before slowly crawling out of his hideout. He returned to the drawers and used his sense of touch to search for the flashlight. His heart raced in his ribcage, making it difficult to focus on the objects.

After some more stumbling through old papers and hefty stationery, his fingers felt a cool tinge of metal. He felt around the cylindrical ridged equipment. He grasped it firmly and pulled it out, flicking a button to fill the space with photons.

Going out the door would risk his reputation. He looked around the office and found a chimney on the far corner wall. His height could finally pay off. He tilted on the platform built for trophies and clasped on the chimney's framework. The aluminium bars hurt his palm. He pushed himself upward and gripped firmly on the ridges.

He knocked out a couple of trophies and sent them clonking on the ground. Somprakash jumped and gave a final push, and his torso had made it through the ridges. With the help of gravity, he rolled his legs through the tiny space and tumbled down to the ground.

He budged his head from side to side, thinking about where fate had brought him.

XXXVII-2010

Punjab

Namita sifted the pakoras out of the bubbling oil as Jannat circled in the drawing room laden with Namita's georgette dupattas pretending to be a sophisticated grown woman.

Shrishti, her younger sister, cheered for her with a building block in hand.

Jannat adjusted her purse wound around her right shoulder. She flexed her vast glasses and barely pleated saree as she manifested the ideals of being pretentious.

"Slisti, thithith how you walk in salee(saree), I learnt it by wathing mom," she declared, beaming with pride.

Namita filled her pan with a mixture of gram flour and buttermilk, preparing to make her kadhi. She added the required spices and peeped to check on her tiny soldiers.

Jannat placed her left hand on the hip and clutched her glasses before stepping toward her sister. She sashayed and made a disgusted face when she saw the mess Shrishti had made. Waving her curly hair in the air, she continued walking.

The dupattas she had woven around herself came loose and tangled in a maze near her ankles. Pretentious Jannat couldn't let technical difficulties interrupt her educational demonstration. She continued walking cocking her hip and blowing air kisses. Suddenly she felt like she was flying, as the tangled mess sucked in her foot and sent her down to the mercy of gravity. She screamed, startling Namita in the kitchen and an awed Shrishti. Jannat sensed something firm stop her before she hit the hard floor. She looked up to stare into the kind but nervous eyes of Bluewhale. Breathing heavily, she yelped out another scream.

Namita hurried out of the kitchen with a metal spatula in hand.

"Oh, she's fine. You couldn't have better timing," Namita said with her hand on her chest as she sighed in relief.

Bluewhale steadied the distraught diva and helped her to an upright position. Jannat let go of her fashion scarves and rushed to her mom. Namita patted her head and carried her towards Bluewhale, "Jannat, meet Uncle Bluewhale. He is your father's best friend," Namita encouraged Jannat to avoid being scared despite their strange earlier encounter.

"Hello, Uncle Bull-well," she smiled shyly, revealing two missing incisors in her lower jaw.

"Hello, Jannat," Bluewhale said, patting her head.

He presented her with a basket filled with snacky snacks making Jannat smile wide enough to draw gasps from a couple of orthodontists.

"I love theethe," she said, giggling and looking at her mom for approval. When Namita nodded, she clutched the basket and ran out of Namita's arms. She rushed towards Shrishti and began sharing the goodies.

"Just because you saved my daughter, you don't get a free pass to spoil her," Namita taunted Bluewhale, the spatula still held in her fingers.

"They're adorable," he said, looking at the two girls gobbling sweets sitting between a colourful array of toys.

Sunshine passing through her curls, Jannat fed her younger sister with as much care as she was holding a feather. Shrishti murmured as she bit into the creamy chocolate. Jannat ran towards Bluewhale and dragged him towards Shrishti.

"Slisti likes it too," she said, pointing toward the mesmerized toddler.

"Thanth you, Uncle Bull-well," she said, looking him right in the eye.

Bluewhale held Jannat in his arms and spun her around as she giggled like a happy bird. Namita wiped the tear from her cheek as she returned to the kitchen to save her kadhi from burning. Her cute little daughters filled her heart's tiny void, although they vandalized her wardrobe and increased the dentist's bill.

She chuckled at her jokes as she stirred the yellow liquid. Slowly, she dropped in the pakoras fried earlier and asked the spinning monsters to help her set the tables.

Jannat churned the fluffy white rice with her fingers as the yellow liquid laced around the tiny valleys she created. They ate in silence, interrupted by little squawks from Shrishti, who couldn't contain the energy generated from her latest carbohydrate intake.

Jannat finished her meal and carried her plate inside, struggling to place it in the sink. She succeeded after a while and rushed outside to calm Shrishti.

"Slishti, don't do that," she instructed her sister as Bluewhale gaped in awe.

"I have this unholy urge to spoil them to my best ability," he teased Namita, who gave him a milder version of one of her death stares.

(Aarav had experienced the extreme versions of these.)

Bluewhale laughed as he ate through the delicious (maybe slightly burnt) food.

Namita tucked in the girls for a siesta and signalled Bluewhale to her storeroom.

"You won't believe what I found," Namita opened her laptop and directed Bluewhale towards the screen.

"That number on the crate wasn't just for organization purposes. It is actually a Swiss bank account number," she said, pointing to her research.

"Holy guacamole!" Bluewhale gasped, looking at the screen floating with data.

"We can't find who owns this account because of the strict confidentiality of the bank. I have bugged their code, so if there is any activity, I will get a reminder," Namita pointed out her bug in the code.

"The computer geek in you always surprises me," he spun the paperweight and read through her reports.

She chuckled slightly and waved her hand in front of her.

"If we figure out the person who owns the account, we can decode their account details and gain access to a fingerprint copy which they might have used earlier. If things go our way, that same print will open this safe too," she tapped the metal case with her filed nails.

"I tried opening it too, but it won't budge," Bluewhale ran his fingers through the wrinkles.

"It is made of 95 per cent graphyx, indestructible material with a very high melting point. Even if we weld it at 5000 degrees Celcius, the case will not budge. Moreover, whatever is inside would practically turn to ash," she said with her chin resting on her fingers.

"Let us hope they use this account soon," she said, sighing while lifting her face from its resting position.

"Thank you, Namita. I will try contacting Aarav and send in the developments," Bluewhale said, picking up his backpack.

"You owe me the coffee brand name," she replied.

He presented her with a dark blue packet with an animated coffee mascot. She grinned widely, imitating the chocolate-awestruck Jannat.

"I knew I had seen that smile before!" Bluewhale tapped the table laughing his heart out.

XXXVIII-2010

Safehouse

Aarav pressed on his chocolate brown beard and placed on his wig cap. He looked like a purposeful businessman in the grey three-piece suit. As an accent piece, he had a small black pouch case. Lifting on his humungous round glasses, he went out to collect his new ID and papers from his table.

Aarav would visit Manish Rathore as a prospective client for his made-up construction agency.

He listened to the clip again, "It better be quick, or you will lose your payment."

He could draw the wave pattern of the word better by this time. He attached a lens camera to the button of his coat. He stared at himself in the full-length mirror. The marks on his neck were visible quickly. He pulled out a scarf and rolled it around his neck.

"All set," he said to himself.

He walked out the door and strode to the car Somprakash had left for them. He started the engine and set out for Bungalow G-35, near the hilly suburbs of Darjeeling. It was the Malibu of this hill station.

He neared the endless rows of flawlessly built architectural masterpieces. Driving along Lane G, he came near the Rathore mansion. Despite his serious demeanour, he was delighted to see the glamorous fountain near the entrance. He showed his fake ID to the security guard who opened the gates after a chat with his seniors.

He drove inside to find a man dressed lavishly from head-to-toe, waiting with his ferocious dog. He shook the man's hand while the dog gave him a rough bark. Manish tugged at the canine's leash and patted its head.

"Calm down, Bruno," he chuckled like a sophisticated old lady with a gambling problem.

Aarav carefully analyzed his speech pattern.

Manish produced his voice from his vocal cords, unlike a few people who enticed their jaw and nose to make a sound. Manish was leaning away from the records registered from the calls. Although, he could have hired a vocal coach and modulated his accent. Judging by his clothes, he could hire people to dry his underarm hair.

They stepped inside, and Aarav took note of his gait.

Manish walked, raising his knee first and undulating his hips slightly.

Aarav would have to go back and watch his airport clips to confirm if Manish had this habit earlier.

Aarav had to stop himself from gawking at the marvel he witnessed. The entire hallway sparkled with the most delicate paint slathered on it.

Namita would have noted how the plush carpets perfectly complemented the gold accents on the wall.

The whole hall was covered in neutral tones and wooden furniture.

"Walnut wood doesn't crack easily," Manish said, tapping the armrests of his leather-trenched chair.

Aarav smiled at the extravagance of the man. They sipped a drink whose name Aarav couldn't pronounce.

"So, what plan did you want to present, Mr Mansingh?" Manish said, swirling his drink with caution.

Aarav put a map of Ganeshgram on the table and pointed to the big plot of land next to Aarey tea plantations.

"My team has a vision for this land you have here. We wanted to build a tea-themed amusement park," Aarav spoke, handing out a folder with more details.

Manish went across the pages, his expression changing with every flip. Aarav looked around the room for clues regarding this unusual man.

"That estate was my grandfather's. The tea company is willing to pay me triple the price to expand their industry. I kept them away to protect my legacy. Dada would have wanted something that would benefit the community," he said with bitterness creeping into his voice.

Was the bitterness due to grief or the drink? Aarav could never know.

But Manish guy wasn't as bad as Aarav had deemed him to be.

"Your amusement park plan appealed to me," he said, pointing toward Aarav.

"Tell me more about your company, Mr Mansingh," he offered Aarav to continue.

His speech didn't ring any bells with the transcript Aarav held.

"We have been building unique structures for the past fifteen years. My father founded the company and handed me the commanding seat a couple of years ago," Aarav said without missing a beat.

"Brilliant research, young man," Manish said, nodding his head with appreciation.

"What would it cost you to build this park?" He said, glancing through the catalogues provided.

"If we start right now, it would roughly cost around three crore rupees to get the park ready," Aarav replied.

"Okay, your offer is very intriguing. I will run the documents with my lawyer and call you shortly," Manish said, sipping the leftover liquid in his glass.

"Touchwood, touch-walnut-wood," Aarav said, tapping on the firm table.

"You're funny. I like you," Manish said, chuckling like a posh old lady again.

"Let me show you around," Manish offered, getting up from his seat and waving his servants to clear the table.

They went back to the gallant hallways. Aarav had to shut his eyes for a moment as his pupils constricted to prevent the glistening walls from blinding him.

"This is my grandfather's sword," he pointed out the weapons on their left. "He fought against the British, although he was a zamindar and benefitted from them," Manish said with pride.

"That's very selfless and brave," Aarav said in recognition.

They continued walking, and Aarav pointed to some pictures saying, "Is that your graduation photo?"

"Yes, I went to Oxford for my masters," Manish chimed in.

"Oh, do you still visit Britain?" Aarav casually asked.

"I went about six months ago," he said, tilting his head backwards and counting on his fingers.

With his sharp observation, Aarav noticed that Manish had begun counting with his thumb, the European way, instead of his index finger. He spent enough time there to learn certain conditioned reflexes, but the accent did not persist. Or he was great at masking the accent.

"I am sorry, I will have to leave," Aarav said, checking his watch and stepping away.

"You better hurry then," Manish offered his hand, and Aarav firmly shook it.

Stepping out of the driveway, Aarav noticed the guard taming the dog he had seen earlier. Aarav received a frightening departure bark from his frenemy.

XXXIX-2020

Green Lawn Dining Hall

Jannat walked through the dining halls clutching the letters in her palm. The aroma of mouth-watering, slow-cooked dum biryani wafted through the gallery. Jannat spotted her gang chatting with their food laid out in a spread.

Jannat rushed to the counter to get her dinner. She stuffed her plate with mounds of food, although she could already sense the bloating she would experience in a while. Arriving at her table, she noticed that none of her friends had begun eating.

"Why haven't you guys started eating?" she asked, pulling out her chair and placing her plate on the hardwood.

"We were waiting for you. Now we can start," Roshini picked up her spoon and stared at her plate with as much happiness as a father on her daughter's wedding day.

"Oh my! Is that how much you care for me!" Jannat said, highly touched by the sudden affection.

They commenced eating, instantly bursting into immaculate expressions of joy as they sensed the flavours exploding their neurological functioning.

"I swear, I hear Beethoven playing as I chew this," Asha thrummed.

"Is this heaven? Am I alive?" Roshini wandered off.

"What drama are you guys reading for?" Shaina stumbled on their melodramatic exchange.

"The life and stealth of Biryani," Asha chuckled.

"The school chef has to patent this recipe," Ahmed said between bites.

"I already noted his recipe. We are on good terms," Roshini cautiously added.

They serenely ate through the rest of their meal.

While returning to their dorms, Shaina asked Jannat about her Principal's visit. She held out the letter and mouthed, "From home."

Shaina nodded in understanding, and they sprinted the rest of their way. Jannat flicked on her bedside lamp and tore the perfectly sealed envelope. Her mother's handwriting stared back at her. She shuffled the sheets and noticed some wobbly letters indicating Shrishti had written too.

Dear Jannat,

How are you? Are the people friendly?

I get so anxious thinking about these things. The school-calling policy does not make sense to me. I want to hear your voice so badly.

Shrishti has taken an interest in Egyptian history. She keeps talking about mummies and hieroglyphics. We are an unusual family!

She misses you a lot. You could've supported her new interest much more efficiently than I. I try my best, though, just like I did with you.

I made Sarson ka saag the day before and immediately thought of you. I might have had a sobbing session, not going to lie (insert goofy face emoji). You love saag so much. Do they make saag in Darjeeling?

Your mother just has questions and anecdotes.

But, I want you to know that sometimes things don't go your way. Sometimes you will fail or make a mistake. You are human, my dear! Does that mean you are not trying your best? Does that mean you should punish yourself?

No. You are precious. My precious little child. I want you to love yourself, accept these mistakes and not be so harsh on yourself. It is a family problem to get tremendously intense over tiny matters. (Sorry for a couple of abnormal genes, insert teary-eyed scrunchy nose emoji.)

I know you are responsible and sincere, and you will work on your academics.

Darjeeling is a beautiful city. While you're there, experience its beauty. Look at the stunning mountains and absorb their withstanding energy. Sip your tea and think of the leaves that scorched to deliver you some caffeine. Look at the beautiful sky and remember, I look at the same sky. Your father looks at the same sky. We all look at the same sky, it might look different, but it is one sky. Sing like Endymion to the moon. Worship the sun. This time, these years, this freedom, will never return.

I want you to make new friends and laugh till your stomach hurts, till tears fall from your eyes. Enjoy life, dear! I was too protective of you, but now you are free to express yourself. But, be careful too, I know you will. It's in the blood! (insert laughing while crying face emoji.)

I love you, Jannat. I named you after heaven. That's what you are to me - My Jannat, My Heaven.

Shrishti has something to say.

Dear Jannatdidi,

I miss you so much. Are you having fun? I learnt about mummies and got interested in Egyptian history. Khonshu is the Egyptian God of the moon, just in case you're bored of Endymion. (insert winking face emoji.) (Mom is making me do this silly bracket thing.)

I am learning Karate these days. My instructor is bothered by my clumsiness. What are you up to?

Sarson ka saag doesn't taste as good without you. But do your best and kick some ass (Metaphorically).

I love you so much, but I also hate you! (insert upside-down smiley face and a heart emoji, maybe a knife for good measure.) (The bracket thing is not as bad as I thought.)

Control turned back to Mumma:

(I told you, the brackets are fun)

Love you, dear!

Eat well!

(I will go scold Shrishti for the ass thing. She grew up so fast. Cliché, I know!)

Your loving Mumma,

Namita

Jannat wiped her tears and clenched her stomach from the continuous laughing. They were an unusual family!

She looked at the night sky and muttered a small prayer.

Things were going to be good, she thought to herself.

XL-2010

Safehouse

Aarav connected his earpiece and matched it with the voices he had recorded during the day.

"You better hurry then," the voice blared through his cochlea.

"It better be quick, or you will lose your payment," continued the trail.

"better", "better", "better", "better".

"bett-uh", "bett-ur", "bett-ah", "bett-er".

He listened to the clips for a while. Somehow, the times he had spent learning the wave pattern of the clip gave him a sense of comfort. The voice, although cold, sounded familiar now.

He rested his earpieces on his desk and began looking at the graphs on his screen. Right then, his phone pinged with a reminder.

He dialled his last called number and waited patiently as it rang a couple of times.

"So punctual, Mr Resoulda," the woman spoke amusedly.

"The suspect lives in the affluent area in Manchester. He works a nine-to-five job at a Research centre. A diligent, impressive and dedicated microbiologist. He has no love interest or family here. Neither drinks nor smokes. He plays golf on Saturdays and has a sitcom obsession," she said in a monotone voice.

Siri should be taking notes.

"What about taxes?" Aarav questioned.

"Honest tax paying civilian. He doesn't earn much at his firm, but he gives speeches at institutions due to the research papers. Those seminars keep his pockets filled," she replied.

"Has he been near the Swiss Bank lately?" Aarav returned another question.

"Oh, I see where this is going. I will keep an eye out for that," she said hesitantly.

"Just deposited your payment to the London account," Aarav said before hanging up.

Bluewhale had sent in the latest developments last night. Manish did seem like someone who would need to hide his net worth from the government. He called the builder agency he had contacted and piled out his plan. They agreed to join the project. Aarav sighed in relief. He would have more concrete evidence for his next meeting with Manish.

He put his earpieces back in.

"bett-uh", "bett-ur", "bett-ah", "bett-er".

He did not realise when he fell asleep on the solid desk beneath him.

Not walnut wood but firm enough.

XLI-2020

Green Lawn Auditorium

Roshini checked her watch. It was 11:59 am. She was just in time for the audition.

She nervously pushed the door of the auditorium and stepped inside. Students scattered around the place, reading printed-out sheets with immense emotion. She noticed a couple of teachers chatting in the front row.

She spotted Miss Zainab and strode towards her.

"Good Afternoon, ma'am," she clammed out.

"Roshini! Good Afternoon. Glad that you came," she turned towards Roshini and smiled warmly.

"What part am I auditioning for?" Roshini stammered.

"You are playing a widowed woman in the '70s. You have to mourn the death of your husband," Miss Zainab said, turning her script and handing out dialogues to Roshini.

"Okay, ma'am," she giddily smiled.

"You can watch the auditions today and practice," Miss Zainab advised Roshini.

Roshini gripped her sheets and moved back to the seats in the alleyway.

The lights dimmed, and a spotlight projected on the stage.

A woman announced the candidate and her part. A junior of Roshini stared back at the selection committee and inhaled sharply as her mic was set up.

"Oh, beautiful world! What is this feeling?" the junior screamed through her microphone with enough cheerfulness to bring back three zombies to life.

Roshini looked away from the stage and read her lines for a while.

"Is this what it feels like to be in love?" the girl continued faintly in the background.

Asha was nowhere to be seen. She was probably, preparing for her part backstage. Roshini tilted to see what the selectors looked like.

A woman, presumably the assistant, shook her head in disapproval. She picked up her water and pretended to sip it. The play's director was another extravagant older lady watching the performance intently.

The selectors did not seem that cruel except for a man yawning with a Samosa in his hand.

He wiped his nose with a bulky handkerchief and put on his resting disgusted face.

"That was pathetic," Roshini saw him mouth to the director after the girl stepped away.

"Participant number: 3015, reading for Jitendra Kumar," the announcer screeched.

A boy from Roshini's class stepped into the illuminated circle and began reading. His eyes were filled with emotion, and his hand movements were perfectly coordinated with his speech. Roshini held up her brows, impressed at the abilities of her classmate. He stumbled on the stage due to his character's heart attack.

The lights dimmed further, and the room stood up to applaud the performance. The frowning assistant placed her glass down and cheered loudly. Roshini joined in the clapping and cheering.

Miss Zainab took the announcer's mic and spoke, "I think we found our Jitendra Kumar," she smiled gleefully and continued writing in her diary.

Roshini swallowed and looked at Himanshu, bowing down gratefully. The Samosa Uncle still held on to his handkerchief, but Roshini noticed a slight tug at the corners of his lips. All the wrinkly moustache hid a beautiful smile underneath it.

Maybe drama club wasn't as intimidating as she had thought. Perhaps she could do this!

The crowd was silenced as Asha walked onto the stage with a mannequin in hand. She laid down the object and stood up to signal that she was ready.

"Lord Vishnu! What wrong have I done," she said, clattering her imaginary glass bangles on the mannequin's chest.

"How am I supposed to live again?" She said, clutching the corpse's shoulders and begging with emotion.

Roshini was captivated by Asha's acting.

Asha looked immersed in the role but, at the same time, not overly dramatic.

Everybody looked fantasised about Asha's performance. Asha shyly bowed down and left the stage.

"Candidate 3017, reading for Bhalu Prasad," was announced.

Roshini hurried backstage and looked around for Asha. She found her friend giving out autographs to juniors and chatting about her current roleplay. She looked like the Beyoncé of the drama club. Roshini gaped in awe at her talented bestie.

She went there and hugged Asha.

"Can't believe you never invited us to your plays," Roshini whined.

"Did I ever stop you from coming? You guys were never interested," Asha complained.

They chatted fervently as Asha's fansite slowly declined.

XLII-2010

Punjab

Namita absentmindedly tapped her keyboard periodically, producing audio that would satisfy an ASMR lover. She swirled the leftover coffee in her mug and looked up at the screen, hoping for a change.

She opened her browser and logged into her Gmail. There was an unread email on the top.

Coffee Delivered!

from: unclebullwell007@gmail.com

to: manifestingchaos@gmail.com

Mademoiselle,

I am afraid to announce that I might have delivered our secret discovery to the concerned authority.

Hope you enjoy the coffee,

Bull.

Bluewhale was incorrigible, she thought to herself. Clicking on the reply icon, she began typing her response.

The coffee tasted immaculate!

from: manifestingchaos@gmail.com

to: unclebullwell007@gmail.com

Dearest friend,

You amuse me with your silly activities. Might as well start a prayer session so that the account holders access their details. May Almighty pave the way for you!

With the kindest caffeinated regards,

Chaos.

She chuckled to herself as she recalled their shenanigans as trainees.

"Mumma," she heard Jannat muffle through the door.

Dropping her mouse on the desk, she hurried to her room. Jannat sat in bed, sobbing with a blanket over her head.

"What happened, beta?" Namita asked, patting Jannat's head.

"A bidhhorsthhith you in my dream," she said between her sniffles.

Namita nodded in compassion, although she could not comprehend Jannat's answer.

"Shthrithi kicked me," Jannat whined, sipping her water.

"I will make sure that doesn't happen again," Namita held Jannat in her arms tightly.

She sang her favourite lullaby. She did not realise when her little one fell asleep. Laying her head gently over the pillow, she covered her with a blanket.

In the dim light, the faint marks on Jannat's neck made her look more like Aarav.

She lingered a little longer before switching on the baby monitor camera she had installed herself. Being a spy had its perks.

Returning to her work desk, she found a bug in her code.

"Yay! She had a lead," she did a little victory dance to celebrate the achievement.

She transitioned into the tech geek and started retrieving data by instructing her bug with commands. Storing all the received data on her hard disk, she transmitted a loop code to refabricate the code.

She grinned from ear to ear as she typed the new email.

Bugged!

from: manifestingchaos@gmail.com

to: unclebullwell007@gmail.com

Dearest friend,

I am happy to inform you that the bugs have successfully infected my residence. Please stop by to clear the infestation.

A buggy friend,

Chaos.

She peeped at another screen, noticing her troublemakers sleep in peace. Shrishti had managed to loop herself in a position that could flabbergast an Olympic gymnast. Jannat held onto her pillow and snored softly.

"We are an unusual family," she said to herself.

XLIII-2020

Green Lawn Library

Jannat sketched playfully in her diary with her symbology guide set out. She drew valleys and hills and scanned the pages to find an empire but didn't find one that matched the verse in the poem.

To prevent the empire from flow,

Wondering with freshness,

How does one draw a fresh empire?

She needed to get into a fancy-pants-modern-art-connoisseur mindset to get this code going.

She swept over to a couple of pages back where she had drawn last time. The mountains and the leaves looked familiar now. She could not recall where she saw them last, though.

She tried to combine the two drawings on a new page.

The tower clock gonged loudly as its hour hand struck seven. Jannat took out her phone, captured a picture of her drawing, and tried to search it on Google.

Google went, "I have nothing, man." Probably because she had terrible drawing skills or the code had some error. The latter was obviously more convincing.

She pocketed her phone and swung her backpack around her head, landing them safely on her shoulders.

The librarian was startled by the sudden whooshing of air. She cleared her throat and adjusted her glasses to scold Jannat. Once she had Jannat's attention, she pointed at the sign and projected her index finger with wide eyes.

Jannat shrugged and put her hands up like a criminal, stealing a tiny smile from the librarian.

She stepped out and moved onto the cobblestone path, scanning her surroundings by edging her pupils near the whites of her eyes.

A junior moved out of the Principal's office, probably heading towards his dorm. Mr Somprakash was seated in his office, toying with a metal rectangle and reading through some documents.

"Typical office demeanour," she thought to herself.

Principal Mehta couldn't be seen from this angle, but the yellow light from his reading lamp was on, indicating that he was reading.

"Don't see, observe," as Sherlock Holmes would say.

A couple of students were seated in the garden. Jannat swiftly walked to the seat near the obnoxious room close to the girls' dormitory.

She sat on the bench and did her clean sweep eye-scanning. Once reassured of her covertness, she bent down to tighten her shoelaces and swiftly got up, turning sideways and stripping off the tape on the windowpane in one swift motion.

The clean, smooth motion just felt like a backpack-fixing manoeuver.

Jannat scurried off the stairs and opened her dorm door.

The girls were nowhere to be seen. Locking the door behind her, she dashed to her drawer and got her runaway bag. She switched on the burner phone and went to the washroom. The ring went whirring.

"Pick up, Bluewhale," she mouthed.

She heard footsteps clamouring. All her audio decrypting equipment was sprawled on the basin counter. The door lock clicked into place, and Jannat's heart beeped furiously.

The washroom door opened, and Shaina muttered "Sorry" before quickly closing it again.

Jannat stood covering her silicon-smeared secrets with her hands, pulling her shirt over her head. The washroom lock needed to be fixed, she thought to herself.

"I have locked it from outside. Knock once you're done changing," Shaina shouted from the other side.

Jannat exhaled heavily as she put down her arms and began packing the delicate clanky equipment in her bag. She sent water running down the open tap to mask the metal clattering.

Her face was sweaty as she zipped her bag, hiding it in the ventilation chamber. She splashed water on her face and looked into the mirror.

"That was close," she mouthed with her palm on the glass as she tried to control her breathing.

"Shaina," she managed, knocking on the door.

Shaina opened the door and expressed apologetic puppy eyes.

Jannat kicked her blankets and tried to rest. Shaina was deep down in her homework.

"I have a new nickname for you," Shaina turned her chair to face Jannat.

"That's so random," Jannat bounced back.

"I mean, that sports bra was firetruck red. My retinas are still recovering from the accident," Shaina giggled.

"Firetruck, lock doors properly," Shaina instructed, imitating Mrs Sharma's posture.

"Yes, ma'am," Jannat said with relief controlling her laughter.

"Do you have any idea where the drama duo is?" Shaina said, turning back to her homework.

"Yeah, haven't seen them since afternoon," Jannat reasoned.

"They must be brewing something groundbreaking," Shaina chuckled, reading through her papers.

There was a rap on the door. Jannat answered the visitors. What she witnessed in front of her was beyond regular human intelligence recognition. Asha stood in a white gown, her hair slightly messy and eyes stained with tears. Roshini was wearing the same outfit with a different hairdo.

Asha said between muffled cries, "Move aside. I need to rest."

Roshini followed suit and signalled Jannat to give them space. Jannat's jaw dropped, and it stayed that way till the dreary twinning actresses made their way to the window. They opened the glass pane and started praying while trying to stop their tears.

"What in the world is wrong with them?" Shaina stepped beside Jannat to take in the two mysterious friends.

"I am absorbing everything at the same time as you are. I have no idea," Jannat quibbled into Shaina's ear.

"What's up with you two?" Jannat asked.

Roshini gave Jannat a disgusted look, scrunching her nose and twisting the corner of her mouth. She unravelled a letter from the ruffles of her skirt and passed on the paper to Jannat.

Dear reader,

Roshini and I are pursuing a creative experiment to prepare for our drama. If you haven't already guessed by our marvellous and breathtaking performance that we are playing widows, I would respectfully suggest you visit an eye specialist.

We request your support and understanding for the next couple of weeks. We will only drop our disguises in cases of unforeseen grave emergencies. I hope you act rationally and give us our space.

Thank you for your patience,

Asha Shinde.

"No fricking way," Shaina screamed, closing the letter.

"Two more weeks of this," Jannat sighed with a worried expression on her face.

"Haiya! how am I supposed to concentrate if they keep reciting their mantras in those Victorian milkmaid gowns," Shaina crossed her arms and pouted a little.

"Let us go to the library," Jannat said, picking up her books and trying to stop Shaina from rupturing the skulls of her mourning friends.

"What is grief if not love persevering?" Roshini said, profoundly shaking her head.

"Oh, from Wandavision, I remember," Asha said with crinkly eyes.

Asha sniffled and rapidly blew her nose into her tissue, sending some pathogens flying through the air.

"She is quoting Vision in a black and white play. You cannot forget historical accuracy in the name of creative liberty!" Shaina scrambled through the tiny gap in the wood as Jannat tried to pull her away and closed the door.

XLIV-2010

Punjab

Bluewhale's car screeched as he pulled into Namita's driveway. He stealthily got to her backyard and twisted the keys into the door to find her snoring softly at her desk.

The compassionate friend in him did not want to wake her up, but the curious spy had the unkempt urge to disturb her sleep. He sat down and wondered for a couple of moments, hoping his presence would somehow infect Namita's subconscious and bounce her awake.

But wasn't he being so self-centred by only thinking about himself? Namita had enough on her plate already. She was working a day job and taking care of two kids without help from her partner. On top of that, she was willing to shed her remaining energy to help him.

He waited a few more seconds, scribbled a note, and left with light footsteps.

Namita,

You were asleep and snoring (maybe drooling a little). We can work on this tomorrow.

Uncle Bull

The birds chirped blissfully in her backyard as Namita huddled Jannat for school. As a former agent she had indulged in ironing her shoelaces to get her best foot forward. Her daughter obviously had to lead in those footsteps, except for the ironing part. Jannat could barely take care of a plastic toy, let alone handle a heavy metal hot plate with an elongated pyramidal plastic jacket.

"Mumma, I want juith," Jannat said, gagging after a sip of lukewarm milk.

"No juith, today," Namita gave Jannat a fierce look. Later.she muttered to herself, 'Juith, really? What is wrong with me?" she said, tapping her cranium with a confused expression.

Jannat gulped the milk in a flash and joined her mother at the bus stand. They waited for a few minutes, and the yellow vehicle honked billowingly.

Jannat climbed the criss-cross embossed metal stairs a waved a goodbye effortlessly like she was Queen Elizabeth.

Namita hurried back to her house and found Shrishti awake. She bathed and dressed her tot while Dora, the explorer, asked for directions in the background.

She shouted, "The map, the map! ' while getting Shrishti's diaper on before realising her little one was silently judging her sanity.

She ate her breakfast while typing an email to Bullwell.

Swiper, no swiping!

Had a chaotic morning. During the training, they don't teach you how to handle overenthusiastic babyHomo sapiens. I might make a petition to get that added to the course.

You are the sweetest Bull. Thank you for letting me sleep yesterday. I owe you dinner, 7 pm tonight!

PS: Swiper is the evil fox in Dora the explorer, in case you were wondering about the email subject.

Don't worry; I still have neurons left.

Regards,

cHAoS.

Namita fixed Shrishti on her baby seat and got into the driver's end.

She checked off her imaginary to-do list while holding the steering wheel.

Jannat dropped off.

Shrishti diapered, fed and strapped on the safety seat.

Bluewhale informed.

Taps, all closed and rechecked.

The cylinder nozzle turned off.

Appliances not in use turned off,

The door locked.

Backyard room swept clean and files hidden.

Being an agent has its own perks. She smirked into her rear-view mirror and put her keys into the ignition. The engine whirred, and she headed to her office.

Namita worked as the head coding analyst at Revolve Studios. They designed standalone applications for organisations and other public institutions.

She sat in her cabin and rested Shrishti in her crib. The workplace was friendly and understanding.

She switched on her desktop and began going through her emails. Her physical to-do list said she had a meeting in two hours, a consultancy with a client after lunch, and she had to submit her team's progress report to her boss.

She returned to her computer nerd mode and began flicking through the reported errors in their recent code. She noted the probable solutions to each error and called in her juniors for a brief questionnaire.

"What stage are we in the medical research program?" she asked her colleague.

"Stage three completed. We need some production value to move on to the next stage," the person replied.

"Give me the production requirements by tomorrow. I will get the payment credited," she said definitively.

Later, she went on to the meeting and listened to their new plans about merging with a Tech collider company.

She bottle-fed Shrishti while having her lunch, catching up on the latest tech gossip.

"Has Google really achieved quantum supremacy?" her friend exclaimed, pricking through a salad.

"Einstein would be really proud if they did," another colleague said, sipping their vanilla latte.

She cleared the client consultancy with flying colours, minus the few untimed squeaks by a bored Shrishti.

She speedread through her report before emailing it to her boss through her official work email account. No chaos could be manifested here.

She picked up Jannat from her daycare, not stopping to make small talk with the caretaker.

She made a pitstop at her favourite grocery store. She picked up cottage cheese, fresh vegetables and some ready-to-make Lacha paratha.

She hurried home and started preparing for dinner.

"Mumma, I want juith," Jannat whined, clawing her pencil while doing her homework.

"I am making paneer today. I will give you juith tomorrow," Namita shouted from the kitchen while slicing the paneer into bite-sized cubes.

"Shtrithi, my teatherdave me a bad today," Jannat beamed proudly, showcasing the ruffly circle on her shirt.

"What bad did you do?" Namita scolded Jannat as she prepared her makhani sauce.

"No, not bad, badth," Jannat enunciated, looking up from her homework and pinching the air with her tiny fingers.

"You did multiple bad things?" Namita mimicked Jannat's pinching motion peeping out from the kitchen.

"Mumma, you're thuch an ithe-cream cone," Jannat slapped her hand on her forehead, showing her disappointment in her mother's communication skills. Talk about hypocrisy.

"You ate ice cream without me?" Bluewhale arrived with another box of chocolates in hand.

"No! why ith everybody thoconfude today?" Sassy Jannat sighed while getting back to her homework.

Bluewhale heated up the parathas as Namita served up the Paneer Makhani. Jannat clapped with excitement when she saw the crispy white cubes of cheese swimming in orangey-golden gravy.

"What was the bad thing you were talking about?" Namita asked Jannat.

"Not bad, badth," she pointed to her badge, now stuck to her pyjamas instead of her school shirt.

"Oh! You meant badge," Namita sighed in relief, and they burst into laughter at Jannat's silliness.

Bluewhale complimented Namita's cooking skills as they cleared the table while Jannat caught up on her cartoon shows.

"Sthwiper, no sthwiping," echoed in the background as they did the dishes.

"This is the fox I was talking about," Namita said, pointing to the television.

"Yeah, why does Dora keep repeating her questions?" Bluewhale scrunched his brows.

"It is and shall remain a mystery," Namita closed the show and hurried the kids to their bed. Bluewhale narrated a couple of stories from Mahabharata to the little ones until their droopy lids finally settled.

They were seated in their hideout as Namita clicked the file she had saved yesterday. They looked through the bug's hard work and got the fingerprint screening and details of the account statement.

Number: XXXXX12X576

Account holder's details: Seema Rathore

Transaction: *classified*

Last account access: Six months ago

Accessed today: 11:56 am.

Submission details: *classified*

"Classified, my foot," Namita let out her anger by kicking the table ahead.

"We can still use the fingerprint screening to open the case," Bluewhale brought out a humongous machine from his car trunk and placed it on the desk with a loud thud.

"It is my 3d printer," he dusted off its edges and smiled as Namita plugged in the printer.

They sent the blueprint copy of the fingerprint, and a latex version of the same was brought to life in a couple of minutes.

Namita carefully picked up the fake fingerprint and placed it on the briefcase's lock. The black screen flashed green in a couple of seconds, and the two halves of the case split open.

Bluewhale opened the top half to reveal a similar tiny black box inside.

Namita picked up the box and cursed under her breath.

"Another biometric lock," she looked up at the cover; it had the same number printed on it. The back side also had a logo.

Bluewhale picked up the fingerprint with forceps and placed it on the screen. It flashed red and displayed - "ACCESS DENIED" in seven segment display.

They both angrily stomped across the room at their failed attempt.

Namita reprinted a copy of the print and tried matching it again. The seven-segment display flashed red.

"What do we do now?" she said, tapping the mysterious black box.

"What are they transporting to need so much security?" Bluewhale said out loud.

"Every account has just one set of biometric details logged in. There is no way we get another set of prints," she wailed.

Bluewhale picked up the box and flipped it; the obscure symbol was blinking back at him. He typed in the logo to his search bar. Several results loaded in. He added the word security to his search, and google gave up, showing him giraffe talking tutorials.

"Try using the research software when you get home," Namita said, staring at the blank screen.

"I can look through the dark web in the meantime," she proposed.

"Yeah, that would be helpful. This is the only tip we have now,"

"I will inform Aarav. Send in the saved file," he said, getting into his car.

Watching Bluewhale diminish in the lonely street, Namita strutted back to her house and hid all the items.

Suspicion and death could search somewhere else.

XLV-2010

Safehouse

Aarav clicked on the email received from the building company. They had sent in an analysis of their plan and a copy of their project details.

He printed out the documents and filed them.

At 8 pm, he called his last dialled number again.

"No activity observed near the Swiss money site," the woman sharply spoke.

"Anything suspicious?" Aarav managed.

"I did find a brown woman in a limo, who went in the bank but came out empty-handed." she said quickly.

"Find out who she is," Aarav said before hanging up.

Aarav reopened his persons of interest list:

Seema Rathore

Manish Rathore

Ganesh Shah

Atul Kumar

Avesh Siddiqui

Satish Sharma

Somya Tandon

Karan Singh

Atul Kumar's directory was a neurosurgeon practising in Michigan. Atul had visited London for a vacation last year, but his parents were from Ganeshgram.

He called his subordinates in Ohio and directed them to uncover the secrets about this guy.

He made his dinner, instant noodles and boiled eggs. Bluewhale could have made something tastier, but he found comfort in simplicity.

He ironed out his outfit for the next day, grooming his five o'clock shadow so his fake facial hair had a better chance.

He received a call on his number from the Head Office.

"Is this agent Aarav Resoulda?" The speaker said.

"Yes, it is," Aarav said resolutely.

"Your mission manager has something to say. I am putting him on the line," the automated voice siphoned.

"Aarav, how is the weather?" a cold voice spoke.

"Clouds have shadowed us from all directions. There is a tiny ray giving me directions. I asked my companion to leave because of impending danger," he said without missing a beat.

"We intervened and got hold of the suspects," the cold voice blared.

"I expected you would update me," Aarav said.

"Of course, I have sent in other resources and anonymously deposited the cash you would require," the other person spoke.

Aarav looked at his bank statement. He transferred half the amount to Bluewhale and asked him to continue his search in a quick email.

XLVI-2020

Green Lawn Library

Jannat apologised to the librarian about Shaina's ongoing rant about the newly widowed besties.

"How oblivious?" Shaina sighed, booting her laptop and flicking back to her bookmarked sites.

They continued researching and working on their report.

Shaina happily printed out their assignment and submitted it to the concerned authority.

They spun around in circles as they moved to the dining hall.

"Shaina, don't you think we overreacted?" Jannat pensively asked Shaina as they walked along the long corridor.

"Maybe, but we can't beat them in exaggerating situations," she deadpanned.

They both looked at each other for a second and laughed loudly, frolicking their bodies about their mean positions.

Ahmed approached them with a confused expression and asked about the matter. Jannat filled him with the ongoing crisis. He joined them at the lined-up buffet, and they crowded their plates while chatting.

Roshini and Asha arrived in their creme gowns. They were still rocking their cosplay with a tissue in hand and a wary expression. They took very little food and piled it around the table.

"Jitendra loved Kashmiri pulao," Roshini sadly muttered, gathering the basmati rise into a clean circle.

"I know it is hard to not think of him. He was such a picky eater," Asha said, bobbing her head as she took her bit.

Shaina, Jannat and Ahmed gave the concerned duo exasperated looks and returned to eating.

Mrs Sharma gathered around their table and tapped at Asha's shoulder.

"Don't trouble the grieving," Asha muttered as she chewed.

Mrs Sharma furrowed her brows and shifted in front of Asha, startling her.

Roshini produced another copy of the note and passed it to Mrs Sharma. She read the neatly typed words and gave the two girls an excellent twenty-second stare.

"Fortunately for you two, we don't have rules for bizarre dressing outside the school hours. However, you would need to produce a fee for borrowing these clothes long-term," Mrs Sharma gave them her diplomatic smile.

"I expect you to pay five thousand rupees by tomorrow. If you wish to borrow these beyond the two-week window, we can talk to the designer," she moved across the hall and disappeared into the jostling crowd.

"The powerful demeaning the weak, it is the rule of nature," Asha aggressively dipped her roti in the butter chicken, splattering the curry over Roshini's gown.

"I guess you will have to pay for dry cleaning, too," Shaina smirked.

They settled into their beds as the cuckoos cuckooed in the blur. Asha had put on a facemask to protect her skin from all the saline tears.

Roshini walked out of the washroom and shrieked when she saw Asha with the white mask, blanketed in the diminished light.

She clutched her imaginary pearls and exclaimed, "Jitendra, is that you?"

"Oh boy! We at least deserve some sleep," Shaina woke up with her messy hair and frowned.

"Will anyone tell me who Jitendra is?" Jannat peeked up and tried to calm a panting Roshini.

Asha woke up from her beauty sleep and took off her mask.

"If your scream was a couple decibels higher, I might have joined Jitendra in heaven, " Asha said, clutching her imaginary pearls.

Shaina plugged her ears with cotton and wrapped her pillow around her head, ducking back to sleep.

Bummed after not getting an answer, Jannat hurried to her sheets and waited for the others to settle.

Asha and Roshini reunited in their prayer session and susurrated to sleep.

Silence strode around the room. The ticking of the clock gets more pronounced with each passing second. Janat waited for the room to go still. She tapped her bedside table a couple of times. First gently, and then strikingly.

Nobody moved. She gently got up and did the pillow trick to retain her body volume under the duvets.

Getting inside the washroom, she used her belt to fasten the door. No amateur mistakes and probable flashing this time.

She climbed up the granite and prodded the ventilator above. Tapping around the dusty insides, her fingers sensed a leather strap. She tugged onto it and pulled out her bag, now covered with spiderwebs.

She removed the pouch with tiny metal trinkets and arranged them like she had been taught. She connected the wires to her audio receptor. She pulled the sellotape out of the little mic before placing it in the circuit.

Tuning her receptor, she heard the voices that were recorded.

(Male voice) What green file? I haven't seen anything of the sort.

Ok, I will try looking for it. I can't promise anything now. I am trying to stay low.

Oh! these cronuts taste so good.

Google: Momos near me.

(AI voice) Here's what I found.

(Male voice)Wow, they deliver it to you now. Ahaa! I was sick of the cafeteria food anyways.

(Female voice) Somprakash! Is that you?

(Male voice)Kaki, you're still here. Where's Mukesh Kaka?

(Female voice) Why did you disappear all of a sudden?

(Male voice)I was scared. After the incident, I did not want to risk my life more than I already had. I am sorry, Kaki. I didn't mean to abandon you, but I had a family to care for.

(Female voice) It's ok. You weren't bound to help us. We were fine. You could have at least left a message. I thought those guys got you.

(Male voice)I should have. I am really Sorry, Kaki.

(Female voice) Now, eat your momos. They are gonna get soggy.

(Male voice)They still taste just as good. I just found out you can pay money through google now.

(Female voice) Did you live under a rock after running away?

(Male voice)Technically, for a while, yes. I hid in a cave.

(Laughter)

(Female voice) The shop won't run itself. I will leave now.

(Male voice)I hope those girls are okay. Wonder how they managed to tumble down the hill at rocket speed.

Ok, I just need to wait till the security guard moves out for his break.

Ah! What a nightmare! I need to shower.

I tried sneaking in last night, but Mr Mehta came in to distribute letters.

I will have to wait for the weekend to try again.

Bye.

Jannat took off her earpieces and let out a shocked sigh. The audio clips were from the past weeks. Mr Somprakash was really more than just his fancy pants. There was a lot to unpack here.

The female could have been Nandini Aunty. But she couldn't be so sure.

There was something big these people were hiding.

Somprakash also happened to be taking instructions from an authority all the time. Who could that person be? Why was he interested in the green file in Principal Mehta's office?

She took a deep breath and took out her notebook.

She flipped the page where she had written the decrypted verses. That day felt like it was ages ago.

Persons of Interest:

Somprakash Sinha

Nandini Aunty

Keynotes from audio inspection:

Green file

Mukesh Kaka

The incident that led to Somprakash's departure

His relationship with Nandini Aunty

Somprakash's boss

All she could think about in bed were her unanswered questions. Lucky for her, she knew exactly where to find the answers.

XLVII-2010

G-35, Ganeshgram

"Bruno doesn't seem to like me," Aarav chuckled through his beard. He stopped abruptly when he realised how he sounded more like Manish now.

"He doesn't trust easily, you know," Manish chuckled like the old-gambler lady again.

"Let's move inside. I want you to meet somebody," Manish tugged at Bruno's leash and passed him on to the caretaker.

"So, you know that walnut wood I was talking about, my wife thinks we should replace it with cedar now," Manish sourly patterned.

"All the furniture?" Aarav jumped in.

"No, just the table. She says it messes with her energy. I don't really understand it, but I love her. You cannot argue with the Supreme Court," Manish laughed at his joke.

Aarav joined in with his fake laughter.

A woman dressed in the finest Benasri silk and adorned with gold jewellery from head to toe walked out to welcome Aarav. Her burgundy saree glistened and jostled with each step, the jewellery reflecting all the light striking it.

Her caramel face sat ethereally on her neck, bathing in the glory from her attire. She looked like a Goddess, with divine powers and great taste in fashion.

Her kohl-black eyes set on Aarav, and she spoke with purpose, "Namaste, Mr Mansingh, I am Seema Rathore," her lips barely moved as she talked.

Her voice sounded like perfectly aged wine.

"Namaste Seema Ji, nice to meet you," Aarav said, still shocked by the riveting woman.

He never expected Manish's wife to be so rooted in her culture. He had expected a silk robe with a chute of another drink he couldn't pronounce.

"Did Manish treat you well last time?" He can come across as a little extravagant and in his own head. She chuckled, saying this, tilting her head back, and all her jewellery made chiming sounds.

"I would like to formally disagree with that statement," Manish crossed his arms and joined in the laughter.

"He treated me well. I even got a historical tour of your hall," Aarav said with twinkly eyes as his sclera bounced with the incoming bling.

"You don't have to cover his trails. His hospitality speaks for itself. It's been two minutes since you got here, and he hasn't even asked you to sit," she remarked with the slightest hint of disappointment.

"Please sit. You look parched," Manish guided Aarav to the plush couch in the centre of the hall.

The couch was covered in dreamy velvety fabric, the armrests as bouncy as an elephant's feet. The emerald green perfectly complemented Seema's burgundy saree. She sat with crossed feet, her hand perfectly rested on her knee, and her chin tilted to the perfect angle. She looked like a Queen. The juxtaposition as Manish appeared like a hamster next to her, dressed in a tracksuit.

They sipped their chamomile tea as Manish explained how he sourced his tea from the finest refineries available. He talked about complex tea-making processes as Seema rolled her eyes and Aarav tried hard not to blink.

"Why don't we talk about your plan?" Seema said, placing her saucer and cup on the fine walnut wood table.

Aarav began presenting them with his project blueprint, now officially approved by an agency. He talked about his company's heritage and ambitions to transform the city's infrastructure. Seema seemed highly impressed with Aarav's confidence and enthusiasm.

"This sounds really exciting," Seema exclaimed giddily, letting her sassy demeanour slide, "I have always wanted to go to such adventurous places."

"Would you like some more tea?" Their housekeeper refilled Aarav's cup and went off to the kitchen.

Seema went into the food area and brought back trays filled with treats that looked straight out of an animation.

"Help yourself, Mr Mansingh," she placed the tray and sat down again.

Aarav took a bite of the soanpapdi, and the flaky, buttery, sweet, gooey delight exploded in his senses. The nostalgic smell of ghee wafting from the sweet mesmerised him. He almost forgot he might be dealing with dangerous people.

They ate in silence for a while. Manish stops from time to time to explain the origins of a particular dish.

"Where's the restroom?" Aarav said, getting up from his seat.

"Straight down the hall, then go left," Manish instructed him, pushing away his dry fruit cookie.

As Aarav got up, he started to see Seema frown at Manish.

He heard some scowling and muffling as he passed across the corridor. The last time he was here, he had done something while leaving. He had bugged their paintings.

He carefully tilted the frame of one of the paintings, quickly spotting the minuscule device sticking it to his coat's pocket square. He did all this while pretending to fix his shoe, leaning on the wall. He later moved down the aisle and dropped his handkerchief, retrieving another bug.

"You seem lost," the housekeeper was right behind Aarav.

His heart slumped as he got to an upright position. He cursed under his breath and turned around slowly, traversing fifteen degrees simultaneously.

"The restroom is right that way. I'll show you," she directed Aarav to the polished door.

"Please call me if you need anything," she said before leaving, her chunky heels echoing through the alley.

Aarav got inside the restroom with a sigh. He took out his collar button and placed it behind the faucet. It was perfectly camouflaged with the sleek black tap.

He flushed the clean toilet before moving out.

The housekeeper stood right outside the restroom. Aarav was startled and jumped with shock after registering her presence.

"I am not lost, Miss Neena," he said, reading her nametag.

"I think you might have dropped this," she gave him a piece of paper.

Aarav checked the page and thought it might have fallen out of his pocket.

He gasped when he opened the white sheet.

XLVIII-2010

Punjab

Namita was not on schedule today. She steered her cars through the highway. The vehicles around her honked wildly as little Shrishtiwas on the brink of a crying session.

She tried to persuade Shristi to hold her performance for a minute so they could get to the office.

She started singing a lullaby while waiting for the signal to turn green.

Immersed in the beats of the song, Shrishti's moulded face became delighted again. She started leaning towards a nap. Namita thanked God as she hummed the tune.

Honkkkkk! Honk! The driver behind them was such an impatient cupcake.

"Can't he see that the light is still red?" she said matter of factly before she turned her head to the front and gasped in horror as she saw the empty lane.

A green circle blinked at her as she whirred the engine and set it into motion. Shrishti broke from her sleep and morphed into the strokes in a Vincent Van Gogh painting.

The tires screeched as Namita stopped in front of her office. Forty-seven seconds late.

In their training, this would have been unacceptable. But now, she could let these minor errors not bother her as much.

Everybody greeted Namita and gaped at Shrishti's new dress as she walked toward the cabin. It was an ombre with a vibrant shade of peach and Fuschia. Jannat wasn't the only fashionista in this house.

Namita checked her to-do list:

Client meeting at 10 am

Medical console problem

Report evaluation

Jannat's birthday cake

She had forgotten to pick up the cake in the traffic commotion.

This was a code-red emergency. Her neighbours were out of town.

She had a busy schedule today. The bakery would close by the time she left work.

She went through her contacts, hoping for some inspo.

Finally, she called Bluewhale.

"Hey, code red emergency!" She screamed.

Shrishti gave her mother pity eyes as she played with the toys in her crib.

"Is everything okay? Are you hurt?" Bluewhale said, concerned.

"I couldn't pick up Jannat's cake. The bakery closes by 4 pm," she said in one breath.

"Oh, I will do it. Send me the address," Bluewhale said, exhaling sharply with relief as he tapped his chest.

"Thank you so much. You are a lifesaver, literally," she giggled proudly at her joke in such a stressed-out atmosphere.

Namita prepared her documents for the meeting right when her colleague prodded at her door.

"Their correspondent is stuck in traffic, so they cancelled the meeting," her colleague informed her, gaping at the ruffles of her Shrishti's dress.

"You look great today," the colleague said adorably.

"Thank you, I had a rough morning schedule, and now this meeting goes off," Namita ranted swiftly as she looked down at her outfit.

"No, I meant that for Shrishti, those colours are vibrant," she exclaimed with her hands, "they give me Miami vibes," she bobbed her head from side to side with an animated expression.

"Oh! They do," Namita's cheeks flushed with embarrassment, giving her co-worker a tight-lipped smile.

She crawled back to her emails and found the meeting cancellation one. The reason for cancelling the meeting was not stated, but they had provided a link to their promotional introduction video. She hated capitalism!

She clicked on the link absentmindedly as she thought of her speech about why capitalism was the worst.

A black screen appeared, and a woman with an AI voice started talking about a theft at her house. Namita relaxed in her seat as she prepared herself for the cringe that was about to follow. The video ended with the woman recruiting this company's locks and security system. It was called Lockit. Their logo flashed on the pitch black background again, and Namita's jaw dropped.

She had seen that logo before.

XLIX-2020

Green Lawn Central School

"For oft when on my couch I lie," Miss Zainab gently swayed across the room.

"In vacant or in pensive mood, they flash upon the inward eye," she bent lower to better see the students, "which is the bliss of solitude."

"What poem is this?" she asked, straightening her back from all the cosplay.

Shaina and Jannat swung their hands up, eagerly waiting for their turn.

"Hmmm, Jannat, you go first," she said amusedly.

"It is Daffodils by William Wordsworth," Jannat beamed with pride. Her mother's interest in poetry had paid off. She could now get back at Shaina.

Shaina frowned a little and gently put her hand down.

"Where did you come across this?" Miss Zainab's eyebrows somersaulted with curiosity.

"My mother has a faint interest in Nature poetry. She always kept reading them when I was younger." Jannat said with a slight hint of sadness in her voice.

"That's quite interesting, which reminds me of your assignment," Miss Zainab turned back to get her diary as the students groaned at her change of plans. A few backbenchers gave Jannat the side eye and bowed their heads with distaste.

"I want you all to research any historical event in your city."

She closed her diary with a snap and looked up at the students.

"Any questions?" she placed the diary back on the table and straightened her posture.

"What is the deadline?" Shaina shot her hand up as she flipped through her planner.

"Two weeks from now," Miss Zainab scanned the rest of the room, but no hands shot up.

Roshini and Asha had dropped their drama routine for classes. Guess the unforeseen emergency was quite evident.

Roshini put her arm in the air.

"Yes, Roshini, what's wrong?" Miss Zainab asked abruptly.

"Ma'am, how does the assignment relate to Jannat's answer," she said with puppy-like confused adorable eyes.

The students erupted into clusters of laughter. The ones outside these clusters just joined in to laugh without knowing the concerned joke.

"My diary cover has a Nature poem, so it reminded me of the assignment," Miss Zainab shook her head at Roshini's playfulness.

They continued talking about the verses of the poem Miss Zainab had narrated.

"The inward eye is a metaphor for the soul," Miss Zainab continued explaining the verses.

"Does anybody enjoy being alone and away from the chaos, slowly navigating towards inward peace and contentment?" Miss Zainab swirled her neck as she asked the question.

"I used to like being alone, to work out my feelings. Then, I found some people who inspired me to live at one hundred per cent. They boosted my compassion and made me more human," Jannat blabbered to herself, although the whole class had functioning ears.

Shaina, Roshini and Asha's eyes sparkled with moisture.

"Oh my! Jannat, that was phenomenal. Why don't you join the drama club?" Miss Zainab winked, and the class broke into clusters of laughter.

L-2010

Punjab

Namita drove her car at the maximum safe speed.

Jannat ran towards her car and lunged at Namita with the same impact as a lion after its prey.

"Ith my birthday!" she cheered, choking Namita and frightening Shrishti.

She tried to lean back to hug Shrishti, but Namita held her by the collar and trapped her into the seat belt.

"Where ith my cake?" Jannat scanned the car looking for the pastry box.

"It already reached home. We need to hurry," Namita smiled and drove home.

Bluewhale picked up Jannat and spun her around before wishing her.

"Thanth you, Bull-well Uncle, Jannat said, recovering from the dizziness.

They gathered around the table as Namita opened the cake box. She placed the lid back on once she saw the cake.

Jannat jumped around the table, her eye-line barely reaching the glass top.

"Ith my cake ok?" She paced around the table, revolving like the earth and tugged at Namita's knee.

Sweat trickled from Namita's brow as she smiled nervously at Jannat and beelined to Bluewhale.

"I asked you to get a boots cake," Namita whispered to Bluewhale.

"That's exactly what I got. The cake is shaped like a boot," Bluewhale signalled the outline of a boot.

"Boots is Dora's monkey, Jannat's favourite character," Namita lowered her head, her curls whirling forward as she thought of a plan.

"What do we do now?" Bluehwhale panicked and looked at Namita for help.

"I will try talking to her. Hopefully, she'll understand," Namita straightened her face and went to Jannat.

Namita picked up Jannat and took her to the table. She took her tiny palm and asked, "I made an error. Will you try to understand?"

Jannat staggered with confusion and nodded her head.

Namita picked up the lid and presented the boot cake. She almost had to put it away as Jannat got up on her chair and started jumping and clapping, sketching a 4.3 earthquake on the Ritcher scale.

"Thithith the houth they went to lath time," Jannat continued her manifestation of excitement.

"But, you wanted a Boots cake," Namita asked, confused.

"Thithith more fun," Jannat said, grinning widely.

"Can I go inthithe, like Dora?" She asked, marvelled.

"I am afraid you can't" Namita sighed in relief and did a double thumbs up at Bluewhale.

Jannat cut the cake and tried looking through the boot for a gate. They ate and laughed as Jannat narrated her adventures.

Bluewhale bought out a cassette and handed it to Namita.

"What's this?" She merged her brows in a bewildered manner.

"Play it," he said, smiling politely.

Namita plugged the cassette into her audio player.

"Happy Birthday Jannat. I love you!" Aarav said with a lot of warmth and passion.

Jannat recognised her father's voice and giggled shyly. She looked astonished and overjoyed.

Namita's voice quivered as she bit back her tears, looking gratefully at Bluewhale.

"He gave this to me before I left the safe house," Bluewhale said, comforting her.

She nodded with understanding and smiled, patting Jannat's head.

LI-2020

Green Lawn Library

"Happy Birthday Jannat. I love you!"

This echoed through Jannat's earpieces as she sat in the library with a school map.

This was one of the most meaningful gifts she had received from her father.

She listened to it whenever she felt thawed.

She peacefully worked through the map, marking her way into Principal Mehta's office.

This was her first stop: The green file. She had to know what it contained that made Somprakash break his integrity.

She prepared her plan of attack.

She would enter Principal Mehta's office from the ducts linked to the main kitchen area.

How would she get into the kitchen ducts? Easy, Roshini was there to help her with that.

She needed to know Principal Mehta's schedule for tomorrow. Her tech geek mother had taught her how to hack into a console-based system.

The computer that Mr Mehta used had a program that tracked records of students. She just needed to hack into that, and the console would be sacrificed, giving her access to all the files on his computer and possibly, his to-do lists or planner.

The last thing she needed to keep Sompraksh busy while she extracted the file.

She prepared a report containing all students' struggles in the drama club. Asha would keep the House-In-Charge busy.

She eyed the librarian and took notice of the room. A classmate was going through the history books, probably preparing for the English assignment.

She went to the librarian and asked her for a book she knew wasn't in the directory. The librarian got up to check her record, leaving the computer unattended. Jannat inserted her pen drive into the CPU. In twenty-five seconds, her virus would corrupt all the files and gain access to the console. A copy of the program would be instantly stored on her laptop.

She counted the seconds, her head directed away from the nearest camera.

"Twenty-four, twenty-five," she pulled out the pen drive, re-pocketing it. The librarian returned with a book request form. Jannat took it with a smile and started filling in the details.

She returned to her seat and accessed the console-based files on Mr Mehta's device. Minutes later, she was inside his central computer storage.

Typing in a few keywords, she got access to his planner.

She realised he had some extraordinary accounting skills after viewing his excel sheets.

She clicked on his planner application and smiled as she clicked save.

She stretched her arms. They crunched with the nitrogen bubbles popped inside.

Step one: Done.

Punjab

Namita clicked on the play button as her phone's speaker recited her meeting with the client.

Namita: Hello, I am calling from Revolve Studios. We had a meeting today.

Receptionist: Yes, Mrs Resoulda, I will connect you with Satish Sharma.

Namita: Thank you.

Satish: Hello, Mrs Namita. Sorry I couldn't meet you in person.

Namita: I understand. Why don't we talk about your meeting objectives?

Satish: Yeah, I will jump right to them. We registered our company last month and

we have been trying to get a patent for our latest biometric lock system.

We wanted to expand our portfolio and get a website build for online promotion.

Namita: That sounds delightful. The problem is that we don't build websites for online promotions. We are strictly writing console-based programs. That's what we specialise in.

Satish: And no exceptions can be made?

Namita: I could talk to the marketing team, if your sales projections are great.

Satish: Mrs Namita, we are currently pre-revenue. We haven't made any sales as we are waiting for the patent. Our accountant could brief you about the deals we are expecting.

Namita: Since you sound so passionate about the website, I can make an exception. I

have a friend who does freelance website building. I can give you his details.

Satish: That would be of great help. Thank you, Mrs Resoulda.

Namita: No worries. I am here to help.

Bluewhale stared at the play symbol, slowly morphing into the pause button as the clip ended.

"How does this relate to whatever we have been trying to do?" Bluewhale furrowed his brows in confusion.

"This company has the same logo as the one on the black box," Namita said with wide eyes and a superior sense of determination.

She showed him the advertisement video of the company.

"Who is the freelance worker you were talking about?" Bluewhale furrowed his brows in unison.

Namita pressed her lips and nervously pointed towards Bluewhale, "I gave them your details."

She turned around and muttered, "I still had to maintain contact with them. I couldn't think of anything else," she elaborated.

"And how exactly am I going to build them a website?" Bluewhale cut to the chase because he knew Namita had only tried to help him by putting him in another complex situation.

"I will build the website, you just have to do the meetings and some acting," she smirked and pointed to her computer screen.

"Why couldn't you just recommend yourself?" Bluewhale crossed his arms with amazement.

"That would be conspiring against my company," she said matter-of-factly.

"I was wondering if the company is pre-revenue, how did the people in Darjeeling gain access to their models, that too fully functioning and not just prototypes?" He laced his fingers through his hair, thinking hard.

"That is the reason I volunteered you. Figure things out as you meet them. That is your job," Namita smiled at him and looked at the dark sky.

There were a couple brighter things awaiting her.

LIII-2010

Ganeshgram

Aarav opened the crumpled tissue stained with black ink that still scared him.

"Aarav, meet me at the Java Beans Cafe at 7 pm," the note from the housekeeper read.

Aarav sat nervously at his table, still in his disguise, waiting for the woman to show up.

He felt a tap on his padded shoulder, a perfectly manicured index finger in hindsight.

The housekeeper sat on the chair opposite Aarav, her clothes now different from the uniform she placed herself in.

Aarav took in her face, and his neurons started firing back and forth. He had seen this face before.

She spoke, her voice cold, unlike the embrace it was in the Rathore Mansion, "Aarav, it's been too long," she smiled, picking up the menu and reading the contents.

Aarav knew that voice as he had heard it for the past couple of nights.

It was the London spy.

He registered her disguise and thought that she had done a tremendous job.

"Why are you here?" he said with confidence.

The woman shifted in her seat and let out a mocking chuckle, "You told me to follow the Swiss Bank lady. I did," she clicked her tongue and got back in her sitting position.

"Seema is the Swiss lady," Aarav said wide-eyed, losing the confidence that he had after recognising the woman.

"Duh!" she snapped her fingers and signalled a waiter.

"Also, Seema is Indian. She is the Swiss Bank Lady!" she enunciated.

"What about the microbiologist?" Aarav implored, sitting back in his seat.

"I told you, he is safe," she smiled at the waiter who arrived with her order. She passed Aarav his coffee.

"How can you be so sure?" Aarav stirred the brown, frothy liquid looking straight at the woman.

"I went on a date with him," she tapped her fingers on the table and smirked smugly.

"Are you familiar with the term low profile, or did your trainer skip over it?" Aarav scoffed and returned to staring at his coffee.

"Look, the man was lonely. I liquored him up. The next thing I know, he blabbers about his sad life and all the women who left him. A grown man with three Research papers published sobbing with some level of snot involvement in the process. This guy is safeee!" she sipped her drink innocently.

"What do you know about Seema?" Aarav scanned the shop, making sure his disguise was perfectly adhesive.

"I am finding out, but she is a tough nut. Doesn't drink and acts like a Mesopotamian Queen," she muttered furiously.

"You look good with the beard," she eyed Aarav and nodded in approval.

"I am married. Use your tricks on another nut," Aarav saw a face in the glass door ahead of their booth.

He dropped his spoon and ducked his head under the table. The woman sensed the change in atmosphere, got up, and paced to the washroom.

She took off her jacket and flipped it inside out. The black velvet jacket was now a light beige. She took off her wig and put it in her jacket pocket. Underneath the straight brown hair, she had black luxurious wavy hair. She did a few tweaks to her makeup and stepped out, now looking completely different from the woman she was fifty-two seconds ago. She did not find Aarav at their table, so she walked past their waiter out of the coffee booth.

She heard the waiter mutter, "Did anyone see the black coat lady? She has not paid the bill," he ran to the counter.

The woman tiptoed in her heels and joined Aarav, who had changed his own appearance in his fifty-two seconds.

"Keep walking. My car is around the corner," the woman said, her lips barely moving.

They kept a low profile and strolled past the people whom Aarav had noticed in the mirror.

The same people who were arrested for the shootings at the Sahay Inn.

LIV-2020

Green Lawn Auditorium

Jannat opened the much dreaded Drama Club door. She stepped inside and felt like she was crossing pathways between parallel universes. The lethal one starts here.

It was relatively easy to spot Asha with her classic gown and an odd group of admirers.

She slowly paced the steps between them, keeping a low profile.

"Hello, Asha," she said in a sing-song tun to blend in with the crowd.

"You come uninvited, yet confident," Asha could not drop her guard in front of her fans.

"I have something that might benefit you," Jannat motioned the papers she had printed a while earlier.

"Is it my husband's will? Did he leave me more love?" she muffled, looking at the papers.

"Yes, that's exactly what this is? Why don't you come with me? I will explain," Jannat took Asha's hand.

"What is this?" Asha gasped as she saw the text in front of her. "I have always wanted to form a proposal for the betterment of us artists," she giggled with excitement as she flipped through the pages.

"I thought so. Why don't you talk to Mr Somprakash about the same?" Jannat suggested.

"That's an amazing idea," I will get right to it.

Asha sprinted clumsily towards the stairs.

Jannat shouted, "Where's Roshini?"

"She went to the dorm, was not feeling well," Asha waved the papers in her hands as she bubbled down the stairs.

Jannat took the shortest route to their room. She opened the door steadily and peeped inside with inquisitive eyes.

No one could be spotted. She went inside and sat on her bed. Tying the laces of her shoes, she noticed chomping sounds in the background.

Another chomp, another crunch.

"Did they have unchecked bears in the dorm?" she wondered.

She reached up her shoes and plucked out her pocketknife. Unhurriedly, she inched closer to the sounds.

Chomp, bite, nibble, chomp.

"Aaahhhh! Please don't kill me, Asha. I was hungry. I know I am supposed to be mourning, but these cronuts, my God!" Roshini said everything in one breath, gasping guiltily with a jam-filled cronut in her hand.

Jannat put away her knife, and Roshini slowly opened her eyes.

"It's me, don't worry," she helped Roshini to an upright position and pitifully glanced at her.

"I don't know what I was thinking," Roshini guiltily glanced and the cronut in her hand.

She swallowed and looked at Jannat, shifting a little in her seat. She said, "This cosplay thing was my coping mechanism. I panicked with all the glitz of the Drama club. When I saw Asha perform, I was stunned," she dove to get her tissue box and adjusted on the crumpled sheets.

"I ate less for the acting method and now feel so useless. I cannot do a simple role," she yawled into her tissue, making Jannat stir back in response.

Roshini sat back, sniffling. Jannat held her close and patted her back.

"Hey! Stop crying," Jannat tried to encourage Roshini by senselessly moving her with her muscular forearms.

Roshini giggled as her hair moved with the wind at Jannat's tug. She felt light as her muscles juddered after the sobbing session.

Jannat picked up the cronut and pulled it close to her mouth.

"Oh! My digestive tract will cherish this piece of confectionery," she opened her mouth wide and stared at Roshini.

"That's mine!" Roshini unlocked her pillow-fighting abilities and knocked the cronut out of Jannat's hold, landing it safely in her cupped hands.

She gobbled it down, making a goofy face at Jannat, who giggled in response.

"I understand how hard this has been for you," Jannat held Roshini's shoulders and smiled weakly.

"You don't need to prove your worth to anyone. Maybe our intuition was wrong. Drama might not be your best shot," she said with kind-shiny eyes.

Roshini nodded in approval and pulled in Jannat for a breathtaking hug. She grasped onto her so tight that she took away Jannat's breath.

"Are there more cronuts in the kitchen?" Jannat spoke through the chokehold.

"We'll have to go there and find out. They make some in advance," Roshini excitedly jumped out.

"Show me the way," Jannat said.

LV-2010

Punjab

Bluewhale adjusted his glasses as he sat down in the Lockit gallery. His counterfeit resume in hand, he was ready for the meeting.

"Mr Balwinder, Satish is expecting you," a man from the end of the hall signalled him.

"Thank you for coming on such short notice," the man seated in the plush leather chair said.

"Good Afternoon, Mr Satish," Bluewhale said, getting into his seat.

"Mrs Resoulda spoke highly of you. I am aware she has introduced you to our requests," Satish offered him a diplomatic smile.

They went on about the design concept and aesthetic of the concerned website. Bluewhale faked taking notes while Namita captivatingly listened to the entire conversation through her audio fixtures.

Satish's easy smile and fixated arguments felt natural to Bluewhale. He could not imagine a villainous creature could be hidden behind his easy smile.

He did recognise his name, though. He had heard it before.

Satish offered him the agreement papers and watched him read and sign them. As Bluewhale returned the documents, Satish looked around for a pen to sign when Bluewhale offered his pen.

He smiled and quickly signed the sheets returning the pen to Bluewhale.

Aarav got up from the leather seat as the furniture squeaked from below and bid goodbye.

He drove back to Namita's place as they analysed the body language of Mr Satish.

On investigating his personal life, they found absolutely nothing. No family, dating history or connections with any alleged criminals.

Namita smiled softly as she read the jittery notes Bluewhale had nervously scribbled.

"As weird as it sounds, I might have heard his name before," Bluewhale positioned himself to face Namita.

"He has never been a part of mainstream media before launching this ad campaign. Maybe it is your memory playing tricks on you," she deadpanned.

"Possibly, yeah," Bluewhale gloomily shook his head and watched Namita pull up her coding window.

It was always fascinating to watch someone manifesting their passion. The way her impatient fingers tapped the keyboard. How her gaze was fixated on the screen as if God was delivering his sermon through it.

Namita looked like she belonged in front of the computer. Whenever he saw someone perfectly fit for their job and highly well-made, he felt like entropy still had time to get to them.

He shuffled through his research papers, hoping to find the link to Satish Sharma.

Namita averted her eyes to sip her coffee several times as she designed the website prototype. She had a fabulous idea of including the locks and safe concept within the website and making it interactive.

Bluewhale shifted beside her. He was reading through his old research, which seemed a little odd to Namita. They were way after all those events. But she never doubted the intuitions of her co-workers. Hence, she extended the same behaviour to Bluewhale.

"Here it is," Bluewhale's eyes lit up like a puppy as he pointed Naimta to the black ink.

She squinted her eyes, taking in what was written.

Seema Rathore

Manish Rathore

Ganesh Shah

Atul Kumar

Avesh Siddiqui

Satish Sharma

Somya Tandon

Karan Singh

"London, it is!" She smirked.

LVI-2020

Green Lawn Central School

Roshini tapped a cook's arm and whispered something in his ear. He gently smiled and went to retrieve something from the giant cold storage.

"You've got some nice relations down here," Jannat side-eyed Roshini.

"All those hours I spent appreciating their food has got to pay off," Roshini said, brushing dust off her shoulder.

Jannat looked around for the ducts and smiled when she located the metal chute's lined with a mesh lid.

"Why don't you show me around?" Jannat smiled.

"Yes. Yes, it is just that the aroma captivates my normal brain functioning," Roshini chuckled and started moving forward mindlessly, explaining all the decor in the kitchen.

Jannat made some affirmative noises and found the perfect time to knick out of Roshini's tour, clocking around the ducts.

She stepped onto the shining counter and used the radish leaves to give herself a nudge. The fingers of her right hand clung briefly to the mesh, which she carefully snuck out.

Then, she pushed her weight upwards, tearing a couple of the radish leaves. Entering inside, she placed the mesh back on.

Moving forward, she noticed Roshini near the ice-cream storage, explaining her favourite custard apple flavour.

Jannat continued down the duct when she noticed a slope. She was heading down to the ground floor. Gently, lowering her body, she crossed her arms on her torso as gravity did its job.

Her posterior felt a burn because of the increased friction. She held her breath as she descended down the chute.

Coming to an abrupt stop, she looked down a peephole to find that she was directly above Principal Mehta's office.

Once she was inside his office, she checked the clock.

According to his planner, she had fifteen minutes to find the green folder before Principal Mehta would return from his stroll.

She put on some gloves she had stashed in her pockets. Looking carefully through his desk drawers, she looked for the green folder.

Disappointment hit her as she finished sweeping through the drawers without any green peeking through.

"Was I colourblind without knowing it? There is no green file here," she muttered as she started looking in the nearby cupboards.

She had scanned every visible piece of furniture in the past ten minutes. No signs of the tiniest green folder. She panicked as she looked at the clock again. It was time to go back.

She gasped and climbed up the trophy holder as she skillfully snuck out through the tiny ventilating space, not knocking down trophies like Somprakash had done.

LVII-2010

Ganeshgram

Aarav adjusted his seatbelt as the lady turned her keys into the ignition.

"Who were those men?" she asked, speeding through the parking lot.

"They tried shooting Bluewhale and me at the Sahay Inn and got arrested for it. How did they make it out of prison, though?" Aarav said with a bewildered expression.

"Manish was talking to some policemen yesterday. Maybe that's how," the lady said, taking a sharp right turn.

"What in the automobile are you trying to do?" Aarav said, panting as he clutched to his seat.

"You will have to jump when I order you to," the lady said.

"Did that coffee alter your brain?" Aarav asked snarkily.

"We are being chased, you dummy," she whipped the car to a steering turn.

"Why do you think I am doing these crazy turns?" she screeched, looking into the rear-view mirror.

"But what about you?" he screamed back.

"I will find a way out, don't worry," she said with fear creeping into her eyes.

They had arrived in the dense, bushy area of the town. Aarav unlocked his door and strapped his hand to his seatbelt.

"On your count," he said as the sharp wind seared through his tired skin.

"Three, two, one, please don't die!" She sped the car forward, climbing the curvy roads as Aarav tumbled down the tea plantations.

Hopelessly barrelling down the thorny hill, he only thought about how his amateur mistake had risked his colleague's life.

As he halted, he stared at the beautiful city, hiding its wonders and terrible crimes.

LVIII-2010

Punjab

Namita emailed the website's details to the Lockit manager. Bluewhale contacted his agent in London to find out more about Satish Sharma.

She went over and brewed two fresh mugs of coffee. Heading back, she rested her head on the chair and replayed all the events of their mission.

Secret briefcase - Swiss Bank Account - Owner Seema Rathore - second fingerprint - Lockit Head - Satish Sharma.

Both Satish and Seema are persons of interest for the principal criminal.

"What if the second fingerprint is Satish's?" She opened her eyes and stared straight at Bluewhale.

"That's definitely possible," Bluewhale thought to himself.

"You need to return to the office and get his fingerprint copy," Namita muttered furiously.

Bluewhale nodded his head and recollected the day's events.

Bluewhale recalled Satish borrowing the pen for his signatures.

"Wait, I might already have his fingerprints," Bluewhale retrieved his pen and carefully traced it with tape.

They logged the fingerprints into their 3d printer, anxiously waiting for a couple of prints to be made.

Namita placed the prints on the biometric lock with gloved hands as her eyes scanned the screen.

It flashed red. She muttered something under her breath and tried the second one.

A glimpse of green, and she jumped in triumph. The second case finally opened.

It had a velvet drawstring bag. She opened it slowly and dumped the contents onto a clean surface.

Bluewhale stared at the contents, flabbergasted. They were diamonds, but not white. They were black diamonds. One in 10,000 diamonds is coloured. Carbon's urge to turn into a diamond has been rare, but turning into a black diamond is even more infrequent.

Namita gasped as she saw those dark twinkly allotropes and glimpsed back at Bluewhale.

"That's what they have been smuggling," Bluewhale noted.

"We need to inform Aarav," Namita managed.

"The thing is..." Bluewhale stuttered.

"What is the thing?" Namita asked, bemused.

"I haven't been able to reach Aarav for the past couple of days," Bluewhale swallowed.

Namita's eyes sparkled just like diamonds as she inhaled sharply.

"We need to go to Ganeshgram," she said as she turned her head to hide her tears.

"It is not safe, Namita," Bluewhale replied.

"I tried every form of communication I could. The headquarters last heard from Aarav when he threatened them to use the pen," he continued.

"How could you just sit there and lie to me?" her voice quivered, her chest heaved as her bloodshot eyes blamed Bluewhale.

"I am sorry. It is my job to lie," Bluewhale could not gain the courage to look back at her,

"I just did what the managers asked me to do."

"How do we know if he's alive or not?" she said in her diplomatic voice.

"If he did use the pen, the cyanide would have killed him before the blink of an eye," Bluewhale replied with a shaking voice.

"Why would they give him a cyanide pill?" she held her head and muffled.

"We would rather die with our secrets than reveal them," Bluewhale said serenely as a tear dropped from his left eye, more pain and agony flowing right behind that drop, accelerating it down to his cheek.

"Was that phone call recorded, let me hear it," Namita whispered, trying to stop her tears.

Aarav, I want you to come back. We have no resources to keep funding you," mutters the cold voice.

"Sir, we have all their access codes. I cannot leave after coming this far," Aarav pleads.

"You have no idea how dangerous this can get. We work for your safety. I do not want any excuses. It's an order."

There is silence on the other end for a while. Then Aarav announces," Sir, you remember that pen you gave me. I think it is time to use it."

Namita gently holds her headpiece, Aarav's voice reverberating between her ears as she tries to calm herself. Bluewhale sat beside her, trying to live with his guilt.

LIX-2020

Green Lawn Central School

Jannat lands in the tiny alley beside the Principal's office. Her body shudders with fear as she sees Mr Somprakash right before her.

She looks behind for an escape route, but Mr Somprakash reveals a green folder from behind his shirt.

"Looking for this?" he says with a smirk.

"Good Evening, Sir. What are you talking about?" She says with an unwavering tone despite her heart hammering inside her ribcage.

"Who do you work for?" Somprakash commanded.

"What do you mean, Sir?" she smiled innocently.

"Jannat, don't try to hide, dear," Nandini Aunty appeared in the alleyway.

"Let us speak in my office," Somprakash signalled.

Nandini and Somprakash sit in front of Jannat. They look at her sternly as she adjusts in her chair.

"Speak, dear," Nandini Aunty says with a gentle smile.

"What are you trying to say?" Jannat raised her eyebrow.

"You want that folder as badly as we do, and you don't even know what to do with it," Somprakash spat out.

"I have a recording, and I am pretty sure you can get fired from your job if Principal Mehta finds out about it," she shoots back at Somprakash.

"How can you reveal the recording without forsaking your identity?" Nandini Aunty glared at her through her glasses.

"Oh well! Technology, you know. I can hack into his database and plant it there," Jannat relaxed back into her seat, "Who are you both?" She channelled her inner evil interviewer.

"Why do we play like Tom and Jerry, kiddo?" Nandini Aunty said sweetly.

"The day I saw you at my restaurant, I knew you were not normal. You work for Bluewhale, don't you?" Nandini said matter-of-factly.

"Why would I work for a mammal?" Jannat laughed.

"Oh! Drop the act," Somprakash steered back in.

Somprakash zipped his lips and eyed Nandini Aunty. Jannat cracked her knuckles and retrieved her penknife.

"I can kill you both and not get framed for it," Jannat smiled kindly.

"Wow, that escalated very fast," Nandini Aunty exclaimed.

"We're the good people. Why would you do that?" Somprakash reasoned.

"Good people would not gang up on a minor like you did in the alley," Jannat stroked the edge of her knife.

"We wanted you to come clean to us," Nandini Aunty shuffled in her seat.

"I know you guys have something to hide," Jannat strode out of the office.

"If you want to save your job, meet me tomorrow in the library. Same time," she eyed Somprakash before shutting the door.

LX-2010

Punjab

Namita removes the headpiece and stares into the void for a while. Bluewhale doesn't move either.

"Satish is our only lead," she says, jerking awake.

"You are still thinking about the case," Bluewhale eyes her, concerned.

"Think about a plan. How do we get into Satish's head and figure out his relationship with the Swiss Bank lady," she deadpans.

The room falls into silence again.

"You need rest," Bluewhale signals her back into reality.

"How will I ever rest?" she held her head down and bit back her tears, "How will I ever rest, Bluewhale?"

"Mumma ith trying?" Jannat taps on the door hurriedly.

Namita wipes her tears before getting to the door. Jannat crushes Namita into a hug and doesn't let go.

"Don't try, Mumma," she says, wiping her tears with her wobbly fingers.

Bluewhale stood afar gazing at the stars, hoping Aarav would look at the same sky, wherever he was.

LXI-2020

The girls' dormitory

Jannat holds her coffee as Shaina examines the bruise.

"How did you hurt yourself, Firetruck?" Shaina says, disinfecting the bruise.

"Firetruck is not my name," Jannat pouts back.

"I know what you did last summer," Shaina whispers into Jannat's ear.

Jannat's eyes go wide, and her face turns red as she decides what to do next.

"Look me in the eyes, my lover," Asha sings back.

"I know what you did last summer," Roshini bounces in.

"So, tell me where you've been," they echo together.

Asha narrates her experience at Somprakash's office while Roshini questions Jannat about where she disappeared.

Asha and Roshini have a much-needed conversation about their role-play. Asha patted Roshini's back and told her that she had wanted to stop the method acting. She stayed only because of Roshini's persistence. They hugged each other and let bygones be bygones.

"I hope this newfound friendship doesn't lead to another role-play," Shaina scrunches into Jannat's ear.

Jannat throws back her head and laughs at Shaina's witty joke. They keep adding details and laughing as the dramatists quote Shakespeare in the back.

"But seriously though, how did you get hurt?"

"Nothing just slipped down the stairs," Jannat said, patting her bruise.

"Oh! Did you guys forget what day it is today!" Roshini towered over everyone by climbing on her bed.

"Saturday Night! Pillowfight night! Big Night! Saturday Night! Saa-turr-Day Night!" Asha enthusiastically portrays.

"Boy, Oh Boy! You're channelling your inner Chandler now," Jannat entwined her hair as they all broke into crazy laughter.

The door flung open, and they saw Mrs Sharma gasping for air as she barged into the dorm and started checking off her notepad.

"What's the matter, ma'am?" Shaina said, getting up from her bed.

"There has been a kidnapping in the school," Mrs Sharma manages before she walks out the door again and warns the girls to stay in their dorm.

The girls take in the information and quickly lock all the doors and windows. Jannat helps herself to an upright position and tries to calm everyone.

"Open Instagram. There must be something," Roshini over directs Asha.

Asha clicks on the logo and begins scrolling through the app. After scrolling through a crystal necklace and body butter ad, she finds a post by an anonymous account.

"This says a boy from our school was kidnapped today evening. Students are being interrogated, and the staff is taking extra security precautions," Asha reads rapidly.

"It doesn't say who was kidnapped?" Jannat chimes.

"No, it doesn't. The kidnapper could still be in the school. We have to be careful," Shaina says, squinting at the post on Asha's phone.

Jannat immediately thinks of Somprakash and Nandini Aunty. They could have very conveniently done the job. Maybe that's why they were acting weird. She wants to tell someone about this but can't without forsaking her identity.

"Asha, at what time did you leave Mr Somprakash's office?" Jannat voices.

"Around 4:20 pm. I returned back to the Drama club after that," she reasons.

Jannat left the Principal's office around 4:45 pm. Which gave the duo more than thirty minutes to execute their plan.

She thought of calling Bluewhale but couldn't do it when everyone was wide awake and anxious. She got up and decided to brew some tea for everyone. Maybe that would help them ease up.

She brought their Earl Grey tea samples and poured water into the electric kettle.

When she held the packet in her hand, her eyes roamed around the packaging, the blurry logo having mountains, trees, buildings and tea. She thought to herself that it wasn't great branding.

As she handed the cups to everyone, they circled together and started asking riddles to lighten up the mood.

"Two children are born to the same mother, at the same time, but they are not twins. How is this possible?" Roshini slurps her tea.

"They are non-identical twins," Shaina says with her burrowed brows.

Roshini shakes her head.

"They are conjoined twins," Jannat adds.

Roshini puts down her cup and says, "They are not twins of any form."

"I didn't even know there were that many kinds of twins," Asha rolls back her eyes and chuckles.

"They were born as a part of triplets," Roshini bit back.

"But at one point in time, they could have been twins," Shaina says, adjusting her glasses.

Jannat's mind rings with the verse she was supposed to decipher.

Oh, the mountains utter in pride,

Overlooking the leaves below,

Do we need to take a stride,

To prevent the empire from flow,

Wondering with freshness,

Bubbling and silent,

The wail pot hums with joy,

As encircled with kindness.

Mountains-leaves-empire-bubbling pot

She looks back at the tea packet and recites the poem in her head.

The verse signified the Tea Company logo. What in the world was she supposed to do with this information? Things had gotten so tangled and cumbersome in the past couple of days.

She whirred herself to calm down and join in the riddle game.

LXII-2020

The girls' dormitory

The girls had gotten dinner delivered to their room. They ate silently and, one by one scuffled to sleep.

Jannat's mind was roaming all around the recent discoveries. How did the Singhania Tea Company relate to her mission?

The enemy had made their first move. Her purpose now was to find out the people behind this kidnapping. She got up and looked for the copy of Shaina's report on the Tea Refinery.

Entering her hideout in the washroom, she began reading. She recalled talking about the fire that broke out there. She dug deeper into the lines to find anything interesting. Nothing caught her eye.

Bummed by her slow progress, she turned the pages. The owner of the plantations had died, leaving no worthy heir. His wife Ayesha had fled with their son soon after.

She thought this might be because of the danger to the son's life.

Which meant there were greedy gruesome relatives in this play.Jannat googled Ram Singhania's family. There were no articles about the same, but she stumbled upon a blurry family photo. She saw a wealthy man holding a pipe seated in the middle, whom she thought might be Ram Singhania. His wife stood to his left. There was another gentleman, probably half his age, seated next to him, followed by another woman.

Everyone was dressed extravagantly and bejewelled in all possible ways.

So, Ram Singhania had only one possible brother that she could track. She googled his brother's records, but nothing appeared.

According to a report about his wealth, there were no siblings or close relatives that Ram had.

Jannat was somewhat confused by hearing that. Who could be that young man seated right next to him?

She had no choice but to contact Bluewhale.

She held out her burner phone and called Bluewhale.

The line went dead after a couple of rings. She tried calling him again, no response this time too.

Frustrated, she called on his other number.

"Hello Jannat, is that you?" a cold female voice answers.

"Bluewhale does not copy," Jannat whispered.

"I am so sorry. Bluewhale cannot be found."

The line went dead after that.

LXIII-2020

The boys' dormitory-same day 4:30 pm

Ahmed rings out of his bed and wanders in the corridors. A janitor with a big green dustbin passes by him and stares at his neck. He finds this encounter obnoxious and continues walking down the hallway.

He walks out towards the balcony at the far end, his steps gentle and cautious. He notices Principal Mehta strolling near the greenery. Nandini Aunty seems to be talking rapidly on the phone with someone when Mr Somprakash calls out to her.

Ahmed felt like saying Hi to her but stopped when she was out of his audible range.

He notices the same janitor taking the garbage boxes to the other side of the building.

Principal Mehta returns to his office just when Jannat emerges from Mr Somprakash's doors. She seems in a hurry and furious about something.

"Hey Ahmed, you've seen Raghav?" Sameer asks from behind him.

"No, you checked his room?" Ahmed points back.

"He has been missing for the past hour. We've looked everywhere," Sameer calls out.

They inform Mrs Sharma when there are no signs of Raghav. The whole school is alerted, and rooms are ransacked. They keep looking at the library, football course, sports room, dining hall and even the gym.

He is nowhere to be found.

LXIV-2020

The girls' dormitory

Jannat drops her phone, her heart racing throughout.

What was happening? Why was God being so cruel to her?

She crouched down, holding her knees close to her chest as she tried to let out her pain. The tears won't come.

Was this even true?

She had no idea where her father was. Whether he was alive or not?

Now, her only link to her father was sacrificed.

Memories from that summer flushed into her head as she remembered when she had first met Bluewhale. She used to call him Uncle Bull-well. He spoiled her with all that candy. Life could be so simple sometimes.

Now, she was stuck in a mess she did not know how to escape.

"Jannat, are you okay?" Roshini knocked on the washroom door a couple of times.

Jannat pulled herself together and stepped outside.

"I am ok, just a little tensed."

"You need rest," Roshini said, holding her shoulders.

"How will I ever rest?" Jannat wondered to herself.

LXV-2020

Ganeshgram

"Hello, Jannat, do you read? Hello, can you hear me?" the lady said, holding the cell close to her ear.

"Ayyy, the stupid network!" She complained.

Bluewhale's research lay scattered in front of her.

She tried calling Jannat again, but her cell was switched off. She stomped off and let herself cry.

Tears that she had held in for the past ten years. Ever since the day she last saw her friend Aarav.

She always cursed herself for making him jump out of the car. She was the last known person to see Aarav alive.

Her conscience stubbled when she heard the cell ringing again.

"Hello, this is Jannat,"

"Jannat, I am Kamala," she managed to say.

"Kamala from London?" Jannat said without missing a beat.

"Yes, Bluewhale is not at his safe house. We lost communication with him two days ago," Kamala explained.

"Where are you now?"

"It is not safe. You watch out," she cleared the dust off her dress and looked around for backup plans.

"They are here too,"

"Already?" Kamala croaked.

"Don't make any move now. Come back if you can," Kamala said.

"Too late,"

"Listen to me. What will I say to your mother? Bit by bit, her family is being torn," Kamala unlocked the door with a firm grip on her gun.

"Ayesha," Kamala stammered.

"Ram Singhania's wife, Ayesha? Hello, do you read?" Jannat screamed.

Signals had ways of dying when you needed them.

Entropy is funny.

Life is funnier.

LXVI-2020

The girls' dormitory

Jannat mimicked throwing the phone on the bathroom floor in slow motion but then placed it back on the counter.

It seemed that Kamala was in mortal danger too. Ayesha could be the one behind all this.

Why was God being so merciful with all the unnecessary complications?

She tapped onto her watch. It was fifteen minutes before she had to meet Somprakash in the library. She armed herself with all the defence she would need.

13 pieces of garbage-looking electronic components that could be assembled into a gun in fifteen seconds with skilful hands. Her penknife was safe in her sock. Her torch could double as a taser.

Six years of self-defence training were ingrained in her muscles if she could not save herself with these things. Hopefully, they will work when needed.

She looked into the mirror and prayed.

For her father to be at peace wherever he was.

For Bluewhale, to be found.

For her mother and sister to be safe.

For Kamala, to be alive.

For Raghav, to be calm and safe.

For Somprakash, to not die tonight.

LXVII-2020

Ganeshgram

"Take away the gun. I won't kill you," Ayesha demanded.

Kamala's grip didn't loosen.

"Really?" Ayesha said with a bored look, gripping her own gun tighter.

"This is how we talk," Kamala resonated.

"Ok, let me inside at least."

"I am not sure you would want to go in."

"I am trying to look for my son."

"I have a lot to deal with right now. Meet me tomorrow. Same place."

Ayesha hesitated at first but left, walking silently to her car. Kamala waits for her to leave before going back inside. She parks her car in front of the gate and grabs Bluewhale's working phone and leftover papers before getting in the car and driving as far as the roads could take her.

LXVIII-2020

Green Lawn Library

Somprakash entered the library and greeted the woman seated inside. He strode with purpose moving down the sections of books bundled there.

He halted at a safe blindspot, where the school cameras could not locate him. He nervously glanced at his watch, shuffling his fingers through the spines of the books, holding a hefty folder in his other hand.

Jannat tapped him from behind and smiled at him.

"What a pretty day!" Somprakash uttered.

"Could be your last," Jannat stared back.

"I have nothing to do with Bluewhale's disappearing."

"But, you did hear of it, didn't you? Your knowledge reveals your guilt."

"What do you want?"

"The truth."

"What do I get in return?"

"Your life.Hopefully peaceful."

"You promise me something you have no control over."

Jannat snapped her boot onto Somprakash's left knee, holding his torso as he fell forward. She had a sharp blade close to his throat that rested nestled in her arms.

"You do not decide what I have control over. Now speak," Jannat whispered into his ear.

"Bluewhale and Aarav were my close friends. I worked in the Tea Refinery. I started as a double agent, feeding your father the information and working for the Boss. Everything seemed okay until your father and Bluewhale were nearly shot. I chickened out and went into the mountains. After a couple years there and the Boss managed to contact me again. He pardoned my life in return for faithful service. I took this job after we injured the last In-charge in an accident. The next thing I know, the Boss contacts me and asks me to get the green file. Nandini joined in my mission as she was lost after her husband died of a heart attack. She has done no wrong, don't harm her. I don't know anything about the kidnapping. I tried calling Bluewhale, but he would not pick up. A woman on that line told me he died and cut the call. She sounded lost."

"Just like that, you betrayed them?" Jannat spoke with bitterness in her voice.

"I value my life more than my secrets," he answered unapologetically.

"You know anything of the kidnapping?" She said, stroking the blade in her right hand, completely aware of all the movement in her 5-metre radius.

"No, but I know it has something to do with this," he motioned to the green book.

Jannat snatched the folder out of his grip and took a deep breath.

"How do you contact the boss?"

"I have his number," he signalled to his cell.

"Leave the city, don't come back," Jannat said as she memorised the ten digits and signalled Somprakash to leave.

At least they were both alive.

LXIX-2020

Ganeshgram

Ayesha sat in her car right when Kamala tapped lightly on her window.

"Which son were you talking about?" Kamala says, adjusting to the car seat.

"I have only one son," Ayesha says, exasperated.

"The one that Aarav and Bluewhale had delivered to the orphanage."

"I mean, I delivered him. They transported him safely. But, yes."

"The orphanage burnt down. We don't know if your son is alive."

"I know he is alive."

"How?"

Ayesha dropped a locket from her right hand. The fine gold was encrusted with a logo. It was intricate and had a little jewel on it.

"This is another fragment I had put on my son before he was taken away. Three days ago, I found a picture of that locket on the lost and found page of this school in Darjeeling," she unpocketed her phone and scrolled down to the post, "See, it was on their website. Then it got reblogged because of the design."

"What if the orphanage just sold that locket when they found the baby?"

"At least, finding the owner will help us trace the seller," Ayesha reasoned.

"Do any of your enemies know about this locket?" Kamala held the lustrous jewellery in her palm and suspected it closely.

"The logo is easily recognisable, so.." Ayesha blurted.

"I am keeping the locket. I will call if I find anything."

"I am coming with you."

"You need to go back to that Island and let me figure this out."

"I won't. I have to meet my son."

Kamala shut the car door with great force and stomped off.

Ayesha rapidly removed her seatbelt and shot through the window, "You think you can handle everything on your own, but you know you can't."

"Don't drive harshly. Your tires leave marks," Kamala said, locking the safehouse door.

Ayesha would not give up so easily. She went to the window and tapped rapidly on the bulletproof panes. Kamala rolled her eyes and grabbed her car keys; she opened the door

again to find Ayesha rapping on the windows.

"Let me help you," Ayesha screamed, running towards Kamala.

"You might die," Kamala hurried towards her car.

"On the inside, I already did," Ayesha discontinued.

Ayesha's lips were pressed together, and her feet refused to move.

"Me too," Kamala looked into those tired old eyes.

They had grieved for a husband and a son.

A son who might be in Darjeeling.

There was a tiny twinkle of hope somewhere in Ayesha's honey-brown iris.

LXX-2020

The girls' dormitory

Jannat scanned the pages of the green folder. It was a register from some Orphanage.

It had records laid out right from 1965.

The pages were old and murky.

What could these pages possibly contain?

She couldn't scroll through more than 60 years of records in a jiffy. She just scanned the pages to find something peculiar.

As she reached the records for 2010, she found a couple of torn pages near the middle of that year.

"Somprakasshh, How could you?" she said, stomping her foot on the tiles.

"We have to meet," she whispered on the call to Kamala.

"Where?" Kamala sounded desperate.

"I cannot leave this place. You come here, meet me as a relative. Do something," Jannat said hopelessly.

"Open the door. Your aunt is here," Kamala's voice appeared to echo in the room.

"Whaattt!" Jannat billowed as she opened the dorm door.

"I am Ayesha Singhania. Nice to meet you," a woman in her fifties smiled at Jannat.

She had the same vitality in her face as the woman seated next to Ram in the family portrait.

"Jannat Resoulda. Nice to meet you. I hope you don't kill me," Jannat smiled, tilting her head sideways as she shook the wrinkling hand.

"I am afraid I have a reputation for doing so," Ayesha smirked.

Kamala opened her briefcase, removing tons of papers and a black velvet pouch.

"What is the plan?" Jannat eyed the two women.

"Let us first form a chronological order from everything that we know," Ayesha tapped her Gucci clutch.

"You go first since you are the oldest," Kamala taps Ayesha.

"I do not like this attitude, but ok. I married Ram after college. His parents were against the marriage as I am Muslim. We had to leave their house and start from scratch. But, what do you know? His father died suddenly, and Ram inherited the Tea

Refineries. He started managing them diligently, and we had a son when everything was going well. He met an assistant along the way, Seema, I think. Very cunning lady. She married a wealthy young guy that Ram briefly knew. We lived like a little family together.

Everything was going well. Until, there was a fire in the refinery one day, and Ram died," a tear dropped from Ayesha's perfectly lacquered lower lashes.

"I knew his old relatives would pounce on all that wealth. So, I fled and asked my sister, Kamala, to safeguard the baby. So that even if I was found, my son could still be safe. My lawyers tried to draw a negotiation, but the relatives did not budge. Hence, I assigned managers and went underground."

"According to Aarav and Bluewhale's research, there is an unchecked black diamond smuggling going on in the name of the refinery," Kamala went ahead.

"They are being smuggled in biometric safes designed by this company called Lockit. But, they have ties with that company too. Because they were using their latest models in 2010, even before the company started sales," Kamala said, showing the records.

"Some guy named Satish Sharma owns that company," Jannat said after a quick google search.

"He is also on the persons of interest list for being involved in the smuggling. The Seema that Ayesha mentioned has a Swiss Bank account that her husband Manish Rathore helped her open," Kamala explained.

"Ahhh, that's who she married, Manish Rathore," Ayesha recalled.

"What about the kidnapping?" Jannat raptly asked.

"We believe that whoever was kidnapped is Ayesha's son," Kamala continued.

Ayesha went on to show the locket and explain the lost and found post on their school website.

"Raghav was kidnapped," Jannat said, opening her own notes.

"Somprakash believes the kidnapping had something to do with this green file," Jannat brought out the register.

Kamala read through the records and stared in shock at Ayesha.

"This is the same orphanage your son was in," Kamala motioned.

Ayesha gaped at the register and ran her fingers through the torn pages.

"Bluewhale had given me a code that unlocks to be the logo of the Tea refinery. Does that mean he was asking me to find your son?" Jannat mutters.

"Why wouldn't he directly say that to you?" Ayesha suspects.

"He might have meant it in some other way. Like something is wrong with the tea refinery," Kamala muttered.

"Let's get to the most critical part. Raghav is in trouble. How do we save him?" Ayesha said, clapping her hands to get attention.

"Jannat, open the door. Let us in!" Roshini screamed from the door.

They quickly packed their evidence and composed themselves.

LXXI-2020

Green Lawn Library

Jannat dialled the ten digits she had memorised into her laptop. The GPS locator could not pick up on its location.

"Should I try calling?" Jannat gently said to Kamala.

"We will risk Somprakash's safety." Kamala replied.

Principal Mehta walked past the library, heading to his office.

Ayesha looked at the screen and said, "We can use my number to call. If things go south. I can just pretend it to be a wrong number."

Kamala clicks on the much dreaded green button.

"Hello. This bett-uh be Somprakash," a sharp voice answered.

"Where are you? I need your help," the man on the other end continued.

"What's with the bru-tahl silence?" the man billowed.

Jannat's eyes went wide with recognition. She looked right at Principal Mehta's office. She made out that his shadow was shouting into a cellphone.

Jannat rushed Kamala and Ayesha to the office.

"I am hanging up if you won't speak," Principal Mehta complained.

Kamala's eyes widened in shock as she placed the voice and accent.

The man sitting in the plush chair was the same man she had done housekeeping for.

She walked into the office and stared right at Manish Rathore.

LXXII-2020

Green Lawn Central School

Manish gasped in horror beneath Kamala's gun. Ayesha shut the doors and windows just as Jannat tugged his hands behind the chair.

"Speak," Kamala registered in her no-nonsense voice.

"I work for Seema. I have no real information about any of this," Manish jittered.

"We can do this the easy way, or I can beat you till you spill everything," Kamala spat back.

"Where are the children?" Ayesha barked at Manish.

"I have no idea. I just assisted in the kidnapping," Manish said with real tears forming around his eyes.

Kamala pulled Manish's hair and punched him in the face. Blood trickled down Green Lawn's Principal's nose.

"Where are the children?" Kamala said, pointing her gun at his forehead.

"Come with me, but lose the guns," Manish signalled.

Manish got out of his office. The three ladies circled Manish as he beelined to the empty space between the library and the boys' dormitory.

He unlocked the large dumpster to reveal Raghav asleep in it. Next to Raghav, Bluewhale lay unconscious.

LXXIII-2020

Green Lawn Hospital Wing

Bluewhale slowly opened his eyes with his vision blurred, adjusting to the light.

"We thought we had lost you." Kamala spoke with tears in his eyes.

Namita held Jannat's arm as she scolded Bluewhale for his carelessness.

From the corner of her eye, Ayesha noticed Raghav startling awake. She motioned Kamala to execute her plan.

Meanwhile, Bluewhale explained how Seema and Manish had found a diamond mine in the Tea refinery, assisting Ram. They caused a fire in the East section and operated an illegal mine in the Singhania Tea Refineries. These diamonds were the ones that they smuggled throughout the country.

"But now, the East section is back to ashes," Ayesha brought over food for everyone.

She narrated how she got the mine checked and disintegrated the entire tunnel. The East section was closed again.

Kamala returned with sad news. Raghav knew nothing of the locket. He found it on the ground and started wearing it because it looked cool.

Ayesha hung her head in sorrow, and Namita tried to comfort her.

Manish sat trapped in the dumpster till the officials held him in custody.

He was their only link to find Aarav.

Bluewhale smiled, flashing his perfectly straight teeth. He looked around to find Jannat and her friends holding a basket of his favourite snacky snacks.

"This is for you, Uncle Bull-well," Jannat chirped.

He grinned even more expansive, sharing their little inside joke.

LXXIV-2021

The girls' dormitory

Letter from Ayesha

Dear Jannat,

How are you? How are your friends?

Asha just posted on Instagram about her vacation plans. I never got to repay your father or Bluewhale for their help. Neither could I express my gratitude towards you.

I don't know if I will ever find my son. But, I have my other children that I love.

Would you like to spend your vacations on my island? I own a small one near Andaman. I hope you will want to come.

Also, if your friends want to stay, ask them to accompany you.

Roshini, Shaina, Asha, and Ahmed.

Take care.

Ayesha.

"Who wants to go on an island adventure?" Jannat looked around the room.

The girls jumped in triumph when Jannat showed them the letter.

"Your aunt owns an island?" Roshini said wide-eyed.

"I will have to ask my parents," Shaina said sweetly.

LXXV-11TH AUGUST 2021

Somewhere in the Andaman

Rainwater gushes around the window pane while Jannat silently stares at the thundering sky. She wanted an island vacation, but who knew she would almost die having one?

"I found some fruits," Shaina cheers from the musty floor. Finally, some nourishment for them.

Jannat looks around at the tear-stained faces, all waiting for help to arrive. Would they ever get out of this place? She wonders.

She wishes she had never done this.

www.ingramcontent.com/pod-product-compliance
Lightning Source LLC
LaVergne TN
LVHW041148150826
845673LV00001B/98

* 9 7 9 8 8 8 7 8 3 5 8 9 1 *